GORDON KORMAN
BRUNO & BOOTS
GO JUMP IN THE POOL!

Also by Gordon Korman
Beware the Fish!
This Can't Be Happening at Macdonald Hall!
The War with Mr. Wizzle

**Other APPLE® PAPERBACKS
You Will Want to Read:**

The Magic Moscow
   by Daniel Pinkwater
Mr. Wolf and Me
   by Mary Francis Shura
The TV Kid
   by Betsy Byars

GORDON KORMAN
BRUNO & BOOTS
GO JUMP IN THE POOL!

AN
APPLE®
PAPERBACK

SCHOLASTIC INC.
New York Toronto London Auckland Sydney

ISBN 0-590-40532-2

12 11 10 9 8 7 6 5 4 3 2   6 7 8 9/8 01/9

Printed in the U.S.A.

11

To my parents

GORDON KORMAN
BRUNO & BOOTS
GO JUMP IN THE POOL!

Contents

The big fizzle

"Come on, Boots! *Swim!*" shouted Bruno Walton. His usually overpowering voice was drowned out by the competing roars of the Macdonald Hall rooting section and their York Academy rivals on the other side of the pool.

In lane number 3, Boots O'Neal, Macdonald Hall's star swimmer, churned his arms in a steady powerful crawl. His pace was good, but not good enough. Dimly he could see at least two figures ahead of him.

As he bobbed up and down at the end of the race, the loudspeaker blared: *First place, York Academy. Second, York Academy. Third, York Academy. Fourth, fifth, and sixth, Macdonald Hall. The winners of the meet, victorious in all events, York Academy!*

Wild cheering erupted from the host benches, accompanied by good-natured, though half-hearted, applause from the boys of Macdonald Hall.

As Boots heaved himself out of the pool, Bruno threw

him a towel. "Nice try."

Boots nodded breathlessly. "Those turkeys can swim!" he panted.

"Why not?" Bruno shrugged indifferently. "They have their own pool. Our team gets an hour a week at the *Y.*"

Boots shook his head dejectedly. "It really gets to you," he said. "Only two weeks at school and already they're one up on us. I sure wish we had a pool."

Silence fell as the boys from both schools watched Mr. Hartley, Headmaster of York Academy, and Mr. Sturgeon, Headmaster of Macdonald Hall, present a large gleaming trophy to the smirking captain of the winning team. Boots and the rest of his team lined up for the traditional handshake, but led by their captain, the winners disdainfully turned their backs and walked out. Their jubilant supporters followed.

"Boy!" exclaimed Sidney Rampulsky, withdrawing his outstretched hand to flip the wet hair back from his forehead. "I never saw anything like that before!"

"Gracious winners, aren't they?" someone commented.

"Jerks!"

"Such class!"

"They've been swimming too long! They must have water on the brain!"

"Turkeys!" snarled Bruno. "Someone's going to have

to teach them some manners!"

"I don't mind losing," said Pete Anderson mildly, "but that was pretty rotten. I'd like to fix them for that."

There were murmurs of agreement throughout the Macdonald Hall crowd.

"Fortunately," announced Bruno with a diabolical grin, "I happen to have the very thing. Wilbur, you're strong. Go get the crate I hid under the back seat on our bus. The one marked *Fizz-All Upset Stomach Remedy.*"

Boots stared at him in horror. "Fizz-All! I thought you were kidding! Did you really bring that stuff?"

"Of course," replied Bruno. "I believe in being prepared for any emergency. We'll mix them a cocktail they'll never forget!"

As the bus pulled out of the parking lot a half-hour later, twenty pounds of Fizz-All crystals were turning the York Academy pool into a white, boiling torrent. There was great jubilation on the bus, and much song and laughter.

Mr. Sturgeon turned to his athletic director, Alex Flynn. "I'm very proud of our boys," he said. "They suffered an honourable defeat and were treated rudely, but they're not letting it upset them."

As the bus turned off Highway 48 onto the tree-lined driveway of Macdonald Hall, students swarmed out to meet it. Across the road, a delegation of girls from the famous Miss Scrimmage's Finishing School for Young Ladies waved and shrieked to welcome the boys' swim team home. The travellers rattled off the bus in great good humour.

"Well?" asked Mark Davies, editor of the school newspaper. "How did we make out this time?"

"Oh," laughed Bruno airily, "it was a fizzle."

* * *

"My boys did *what?*" Mr. Sturgeon exclaimed into the telephone.

The call had been waiting for him when he entered his office. "Mr. Hartley of York Academy, sir," his secretary had told him. "He seems very upset."

"Surely, Hartley, you don't believe that . . . An empty crate of Fizz-All? How peculiar. What did it do to the water? . . . That bad, was it? . . . Now see here, Hartley, my boys went straight to the locker room after that disgusting snub, and straight to the bus after that . . . No, I do *not* think the crate got up and walked. I simply cannot understand how you can accuse my boys of sabotaging your pool. There is absolutely no proof . . . Is that right? Well, why don't you try drinking some of your pool water. Perhaps it will settle your stomach!"

Angrily he slammed down the receiver and sat for a moment to compose himself. An odd smile crept over his thin face, and he buzzed his secretary on the intercom. "Mrs. Davis, please send for Bruno Walton and Melvin O'Neal immediately."

* * *

In room 306 of Dormitory 3, Bruno Walton and Boots O'Neal lazed at their desks, picking at their homework.

"So you came in fourth," Bruno was saying. "So what?"

"It's not that," Boots muttered miserably.

"You're afraid we'll get into trouble for fizzing up their stupid pool?"

"No, that's not it either," protested Boots.

"Then what is it? You've been sulking ever since we got back to the Hall."

"It's nothing — maybe."

"Will you spit it out?" Bruno demanded.

"Well, you know my dad," began Boots slowly. "He's a super athlete. He was even an Olympic swimmer once. Well, he thinks the athletic program at Macdonald Hall isn't good enough. Lately he's been thinking about sending me to York Academy."

Bruno emitted a startled howl of protest. *"What?* But — but you can't! You'd be a turkey! A York turkey! You just can't!"

"I may have to," said Boots, "if that's what my folks decide. They know the Hall is the best academic school, but they say there's more to a guy's education than just books."

"But — but you'd play against me on the hockey team!" protested Bruno. "And you'd have to live over there! My new roommate would probably snore!"

"Well, maybe it won't happen," Boots offered hopefully.

"You can bet your track shorts it won't happen," Bruno snapped, "because we're going to get a pool for Macdonald Hall!"

"We?" shrieked Boots. "As in you and me?"

"And a lot of other guys."

"How? The Fish said the budget — "

"Don't bother me with details. We're getting a pool and that's that."

They were interrupted by a knock at the door. Boots opened it and took a note from the office messenger. It read: *Bruno Walton and Melvin O'Neal are to present themselves at Mr. Sturgeon's office immediately.*

"That didn't take long," Boots commented glumly.

Bruno nodded. "The turkeys must be up to their ears in foam by now. I wonder how The Fish knew it was us."

"Lucky guess?" Boots grinned, but his expression held a certain dread. "I wonder how mad he is," he added as they walked down the marble corridor which led to the Headmaster's office.

Bruno smiled confidently. "Not half as mad as Mr.

Heartless and his turkeys," he said. "Besides, I wanted to see The Fish anyway. There's a little matter of something lacking around here."

Boots groaned softly. "Bruno, while he's bawling us out is no time to start asking for favours."

"Just leave everything to me," Bruno assured him.

Mrs. Davis, smiling sympathetically, opened the heavy oak door lettered *HEADMASTER* and ushered them inside. Automatically they seated themselves on the hard wooden bench that was reserved for boys who had been called to the office under a cloud.

Mr. Sturgeon was not nicknamed "The Fish" merely because of his name. The coldness of his grey eyes was exaggerated by his steel-rimmed glasses, giving him an unblinking, fishy stare. He now turned this look upon Bruno and Boots.

"I don't suppose I need tell you what happened at York Academy immediately after we left," he said.

Bruno shifted uncomfortably. "I guess we already know, sir," he replied.

"That was extremely poor sportsmanship," the Headmaster went on. "Surely the students of Macdonald Hall know how to lose graciously."

"I guess, sir, when they refused to shake hands with our team we lost control of ourselves," Bruno admitted.

"And you just happened to have a crate of Fizz-All with you," Mr. Sturgeon remarked acidly. "No doubt all swim teams carry mass quantities of stomach remedy with them." His eyes grew even colder. "You boys took the Fizz-All for the specific purpose of damaging the York swimming pool, didn't you?"

"Oh, no, sir," protested Boots in dismay. "That is — "

"Sir," Bruno interjected earnestly, "Elmer Drimsdale calculates that in five days their pool will be as good as new. You know Elmer is never wrong."

Mr. Sturgeon coughed. "I am delighted to hear that. I should hate to have to approach your parents with a bill for the repair costs. Because this is your first offence, this year at least, your punishment will be light — one week confined to your room after dinner."

"Yes, sir," said Boots. "Thank you, sir."

"Sir," said Bruno, "may we speak with you while we're on the subject of pools?"

"Very well. What is it, Walton?"

"Sir, is there any chance at all that we'll get a pool?"

"I'm afraid not," replied the Headmaster, folding his hands in front of him. "We had one planned for this year, but construction costs being what they are, the budget was twenty-five thousand dollars short. I would like to have one because it would fill a gap in our athletic program and provide some fine recreation. However, these things can't be helped. There simply is not enough money."

"Yes, sir," chorused Bruno and Boots.

"Dismissed," said Mr. Sturgeon, waving them out.

As they were walking back to their dormitory, Boots could stand his roommate's silence no longer. "Bruno," he pleaded, "stop it! I don't like that look on your face."

"There's no look on my face," insisted Bruno, much too softly. "I'm just thinking, that's all."

"About what?" Boots demanded suspiciously.

"About how badly we'll beat those York turkeys at the next swim meet. Which, incidentally, is going to be held at our pool —a bigger and better one than theirs."

"Our pool? The Fish just said we aren't getting one!"

"Yes," Bruno continued, unheeding. "We're not taking any more guff from those turkeys, and we're not losing you — or anybody else, for that matter — to York Academy. We're going to raise the money."

"Bruno, you're talking about twenty-five G's!"

"If that's what it takes, that's what we'll get," Bruno assured him. "Tomorrow morning at breakfast I want you to round up five or six guys — let's say two from each dorm. We'll meet at lunch and set ourselves up as a fund-raising committee."

"But Bruno — "

"Don't argue with me. You don't want to be a York turkey, do you?"

"I wasn't arguing," replied Boots meekly. "I just want to know who I should pick."

"Well, let's see," said Bruno thoughtfully. "We'll need Elmer Drimsdale. He's a genius. And Mark Davies. We may need the print shop. Chris Talbot would be good — we'll need some art work. And get Wilbur Hackenschleimer in case there's anything heavy to carry. That should do it."

"What will you be doing while I'm recruiting?" asked Boots.

"Sleeping in, of course. You know I never get up for breakfast."

*　*　*

"Mrs. Davis," Mr. Sturgeon instructed his secretary, "please notify Mr. Hartley of York Academy that his swimming pool will be back to normal in five days' time." He smiled thinly. "Tell him I have it on the highest scientific authority."

Only twenty-five G's?

"Time to get up," announced Boots.

A lump under the blue blanket stirred slightly. "It's the middle of the night," it mumbled plaintively.

"It's twenty to nine. You know how Mr. Stratton freaks out when someone is late for math class."

Bruno Walton's dark, tousled head appeared from under the covers. "You know I never get up before quarter to, so don't disturb me. I'm going back to sleep." The head disappeared again.

Five minutes and forty winks later, Bruno bounded out of bed and tore through the room like a whirlwind. Within five minutes, the two boys were headed towards their first class, Bruno hopping on one foot as he tied the other shoe.

* * *

At a secluded table in the lunchroom sat six boys. Along

with Bruno and Boots from Dormitory 3 were Mark Davies, editor of the school newspaper, and the eccentrically brilliant Elmer Drimsdale, both from Dormitory 2. Dormitory 1 was represented by Chris Talbot, a talented art student, and Wilbur Hackenschleimer, an amateur weightlifter and a whiz at woodworking and metal shop. Bruno, seated at the head of the table, had obviously appointed himself chairman of the committee.

He cleared his throat. "I suppose you're wondering why I've called you all here today," he began impressively.

Nobody answered.

"All right, I'll tell you," he said. "And frankly, I don't see how any of you can even swallow your lunch!"

"I'm hungry!" protested Wilbur Hackenschleimer, his mouth full of meatloaf.

Bruno pounded the table so hard that one of Wilbur's baked potatoes rolled off his tray and onto the floor. The big boy scrambled to retrieve it.

"How can you think of food at a time like this?" Bruno hollered. "This is the darkest hour in the history of Macdonald Hall! Our world is crumbling around us!"

"You'll have to excuse my friend," interrupted Boots, before Bruno could go into detail about the tragedy that had overtaken them. "He gets very emotional sometimes. What he's trying to say is that York Academy has a pool and we don't."

"Right," said Bruno. "But there's more to it than

that. We stand to lose valuable students — *him* for one"
— he pointed at Boots — "if the athletic department
here doesn't start to move."

Mark Davies nodded. "Pete Anderson's dad has been
talking about taking him out of the Hall."

"You see?" exclaimed Bruno triumphantly. "We
need that pool, and to get it we need twenty-five
thousand dollars. And here's how we're going to raise
it."

"We're going to rob a bank?" suggested Chris
Talbot.

"I've been telling him it can't be done," agreed Boots.
"Twenty-five thousand dollars!"

"A fine bunch you turned out to be," said Bruno in
disgust. "If you're content to lose our swim meets *and*
our students to York Academy — and to have them
looking down their noses at us — then go ahead. I'll get
somebody else to help."

"Well, when you put it that way," said Mark, "I
guess I'll help you do whatever it is you're going to do
— even if it can't be done."

"Me too," put in Elmer.

"Same here," said Chris.

At the end of the table Wilbur Hackenschleimer was
attacking a huge piece of lemon meringue pie. "I'm in,"
he mumbled. "I'll do anything you want, just so long as
I don't get arrested, expelled or starved."

Bruno beamed. "Good. Wait for me in your rooms

after classes. I'll come around with your assignments."

One by one the boys finished their lunch and left the dining room, until only Bruno and Boots remained at the table.

"Have you got a plan," asked Boots, "or were you just bluffing?"

"Certainly I have a plan. I just wanted to talk it over with you first. We're going to have a rummage sale on Saturday."

"Did The Fish give permission?"

"It's possible that he would if he knew about it. As it happens, he doesn't. But I'm sure he won't mind when he finds out it's for the pool."

"What's my job?" asked Boots.

"You and I are in charge of Dormitory 3," said Bruno. "You're also vice-president of the fund-raising committee. We have to dig up salable goods from our dorm, and from Scrimmage's. The girls will be able to get us tons of stuff. I'll take Sturgeon's. Mrs. Sturgeon is always glad to help out."

"We've got classes to think about," Boots reminded him.

"Well, we won't let that interfere," Bruno replied.

Boots shrugged. "You're the boss. We'd better get cracking."

* * *

Bruno glanced with an appraiser's eye over Mark Davies' room. "Take that lamp, for instance," he said. "It isn't doing anything over there." He unplugged the small lamp and placed it in a vacant corner of the room. "We'll sell it."

"How can you sell that?" protested Mark. "It belongs to the school."

"Well," Bruno replied, "the money that we'll get for it goes to the school." Mark nodded reluctantly at the undeniable logic. "Now, let's see what else you've got." While Mark stood open-mouthed, Bruno began going through drawers. "There. You never use that pocket knife." He tossed it into the corner with the lamp. "And that stuffed bear. Now, really!"

When Bruno had finished ransacking the room, in the corner with the lamp, the knife and the bear were a nutcracker, a poster of Phil Esposito, a pair of nearly-new gym shorts, a paperweight in the shape of a carrot, and an assortment of old comic books.

"Now, that's how it's done," he said. "You're to go to every kid in this dorm with an even-numbered room and get all his stuff."

Mark scratched his head. "Gee, I don't know, Bruno —"

"Pool!" interrupted Bruno.

"Oh, all right. I'll try."

* * *

"Elm, I'm relying heavily on you," said Bruno, glancing around the room which at one time he had shared with Elmer. "What have you got for the rummage sale?"

"My Junior Science books?" Elmer suggested hopefully.

"Well, all right," agreed Bruno without too much enthusiasm. "What else?"

Elmer thought hard, closing his owl-like eyes behind his large glasses. "I have some pamphlets on west coast fisheries," he offered.

"Elmer, you're killing me!" Bruno groaned. "Haven't you got anything that an ordinary human being would be interested in?"

"I could sell some of my goldfish," Elmer said meekly.

Bruno thought it over. "Elmer, you're a genius! Get jars from the kitchen for them. What else?"

"Miniature ant colonies," said Elmer, his spirits on the rise. "I could use jars for them too."

"Tremendous!" Bruno approved. "You get onto that right away, and start scrounging from all the odd-numbered rooms in this dorm. We've only got four days to the sale."

"I will," Elmer promised. "You won't be sorry you picked me."

* * *

"We're having a rummage sale on Saturday," Bruno informed Chris Talbot. "I'll need a poster for each dorm, four for the highway and one for Scrimmage's."

Chris, very cool and businesslike, wrote the order down. "Anything else?"

"As a matter of fact there is. You're in charge of gathering stuff for the sale from the odd-numbered rooms in this dorm. Wilbur will take the evens. You have a lot of art to do, so you'd better get help."

"Will do," said Chris.

* * *

"What if nobody wants to give me anything for the sale?" asked Wilbur Hackenschleimer timidly.

Bruno looked the big boy up and down. "*I* wouldn't refuse you," he said. "Convince them. Also, you're so great at industrial arts that Mr. Lautrec is crazy about you. Get all last year's projects that are good enough to sell. The more we sell, the more we make."

"Well, I'll try," agreed Wilbur uncertainly.

* * *

"Boots!" shouted Bruno. "Boots! Open the door!"

"Well, I can't exactly," called Boots's voice from inside room 306. "There's too much stuff. We'll have to get out of the habit of using the door till after the sale.

I'll open the window for you."

Bruno went around the outside of the grey stone building and hoisted himself up through the open window. The sight that met his eyes amazed him. In little more than an hour Boots had managed to collect enough odds and ends to satisfy a junk dealer's dream. There were chairs, stools and small tables, books and framed pictures, battered luggage, an assortment of jack-knives, fishing lures and other great treasures. A collection of the canned and packaged treats each boy had brought from home topped the pile.

"Wow!" said Bruno admiringly. "You really *don't* want to be a turkey! If all the guys do as well as this, we'll have the money in no time at all!"

"Aren't you getting a little carried away?" asked Boots. "I mean, who's going to give you twenty-five G's for this junk?"

"You'll see," promised Bruno. "I guess I'd better go through my stuff and see what I have to offer."

"Oh," said Boots airily, "I did that already."

"You *what?*"

"Subject to your approval, of course," Boots compromised hastily. He pointed to a pile of objects standing on an old chair. "That's all yours."

Bruno sat down and began to go through his things. "How can you give away my track shoes?" he cried in protest. "I'll bet you didn't give away *your* track shoes. And — and my lucky penny!" He held up a large, ugly, imitation-silver four-leaf clover with a penny stuck in the centre. "It's my good luck piece! Do you want me to *die?*"

"Bruno, lots of guys are giving up things they like so the sale can be a success. The least you can do is give up your lousy penny for the cause. Don't *you* want a pool?"

"Oh, all right," Bruno growled.

"What's next?" Boots asked. "Mrs. Sturgeon's?"

"No. I'm saving her for the last, to cut down on the chances of The Fish hearing about it. Tonight after lights-out we go to Scrimmage's."

* * *

A few minutes after midnight the window of room 306 silently slid open and two shadowy figures jumped to the ground. Bruno Walton and Boots O'Neal were on the move. They stole across the deserted campus, dashed across the road and clambered over the wrought-iron fence which surrounded Miss Scrimmage's Finishing School for Young Ladies.

Bruno picked up a handful of gravel and threw it at a second floor window. There was a scrambling sound and high-pitched giggling; then two heads, one fair, one dark, appeared at the window. Bruno and Boots shinnied up the drainpipe and were helped across the sill and into the room.

"Hi there," blonde Diane Grant greeted them.

"What's new? We haven't seen much of you lately."

"We've been busy," Bruno explained.

"He's been busy," Boots amended. "And he's got the whole school in an uproar this time."

"Oh, good!" exclaimed dark-haired Cathy Burton. "Can we get in on it?"

"As a matter of fact, that's a good idea," said Bruno, as though it had never occurred to him before. "We're trying to raise a little money."

"Fair enough," said Cathy. "How much?"

"Twenty-five thousand."

Cathy pointed to the window. "Out!"

"No, wait a minute," soothed Bruno. "Listen to the story. We're losing all our swim meets to York Academy. And we'll keep on losing them until we have a pool of our own. So we're having a rummage sale on Saturday to raise the money. We need things to sell — you girls should be able to dig up all sorts of neat stuff."

"We also need you to talk it up," added Boots, "so the girls will come over and be customers."

"Sounds like fun," agreed Cathy. "We'll do it."

"Be greedy," Bruno advised. "We need lots of things. We're going to have posters on the highway, so we're expecting plenty of customers. Don't forget, Saturday — starting at noon. We'll be over Friday night to pick up the stuff."

"Should we tell Miss Scrimmage?" asked Diane.

"Not yet," said Bruno. "We don't want The Fish to

20

know he's having a rummage sale until it's already in progress."

Boots swung a leg over the window ledge. "Happy hunting."

The two boys slid down and made their way home through the night.

Everything must go

So it happened that when Mr. Sturgeon and his wife were driving home from a shopping expedition on Saturday afternoon they saw a sign which read: *Giant Rummage Sale! Macdonald Hall, 3 Miles.*

The Headmaster jammed on the brakes so suddenly that only the seat belts saved them from going through the windshield.

"William, what on earth — " exclaimed Mrs. Sturgeon.

"I have no idea," her husband said coldly. "I can only hope there is another Macdonald Hall."

"Oh, that," said Mrs. Sturgeon with a little laugh.

"You mean you *knew?*"

"Well, yes," she replied. "The boys came to me for rummage. I can't see any harm in their having a rummage sale to raise money for the swimming pool."

"Why didn't they come and ask me for permission?" the Headmaster demanded angrily.

"Don't be silly, dear," she replied airily. "You know perfectly well you'd have said no. Those boys aren't stupid."

Mr. Sturgeon stomped out of the car, pulled up the sign and tossed it into the trunk. "That's the end of that," he declared firmly.

His wife just smiled. A little farther along she noticed another of Chris Talbot's signs coming up on the right. "That little light on the dashboard," she said hastily, "the one that says 'oil.' It's been flickering. Perhaps you'd better keep an eye on it."

With one anxious eye on the dashboard and the other watching the road, Mr. Sturgeon failed to see the sign. It read: *Don't Miss It! Macdonald Hall Rummage Sale, 1 Mile.*

*   *   *

Behind the cash box Bruno Walton took in money and surveyed the campus with great satisfaction. Cars were parked on both sides of the long driveway and along the soft shoulder of the highway, and the sales tables were crowded with people. Bruno had a right to be pleased. His rummage sale had attracted not only the staff and students from both Macdonald Hall and Miss Scrimmage's, but also a good deal of passing trade. There were older people who had been out for a leisurely drive, young people with small children, and many of the families from neighbouring farms and villages. Bruno was doubly happy, for safe and warm in his pocket was his lucky penny — a bargain buy at only thirty-five cents.

Because there were so many small children, Elmer Drimsdale's goldfish and ant colonies were the hit of the sale at one dollar apiece. The enterprising Mark Davies had printed up sheets entitled "The Care and Feeding of your Goldfish" and "How to Care for your Ant Colony." These were selling for an additional ten cents and contained as much technical information as Mark knew, mainly, "Don't take your fish out of water" and "Don't put your ants in water."

No one had thought to put price tags on the merchandise, but Bruno had quickly made up for that by writing "Price Catalogue" on a blank notebook and studiously pretending to look up each item as it was brought to the cash table. Bruno was very agreeable, though, and if a customer complained that the price was too high, he happily dropped it because, as he explained, "Everything must go."

Cathy Burton hurried up to the cash table. "Well, we've sold all the jewellery," she announced happily. "We even sold the tablecloth."

"Boots will be thrilled," replied Bruno. "That was the sheet off his bed."

"How are we doing?"

"We've got a fortune here!" Bruno exclaimed. He

pointed to the crowd. "Look. I can see somebody coming with that hideous lamp you girls brought. We should have saved our breakfast garbage! People will buy anything!"

The crowd parted to make way for Miss Scrimmage who was carrying a garishly painted hurricane lamp in her arms.

"It seems a shame to make her pay for it," Cathy commented. "She already bought it once."

Bruno's head whipped around. "You mean it's *hers?*"

Cathy shrugged. "We liberated it from her sitting room."

It was too late for Bruno to say anything else. Miss Scrimmage was upon him.

"Dear boy, I can't tell you how pleased I am at finding this marvellous antique," she gushed. "It's a perfect match for one I already have. What are you asking for it, and wherever did you find it?"

Bruno looked around desperately. Cathy had drifted off into the crowd. "W-would two dollars be too much?" he stammered.

"Dear boy, you'll never make money if you're not a better businessman. Here is ten dollars, and I'm happy to pay it." She handed him two five-dollar bills.

Boots came running up as Miss Scrimmage moved away. "The Fish is here!" he announced.

"Those girls!" Bruno gasped, half in laughter, half in tears. "They swiped Miss Scrimmage's lamp and she just gave me ten dollars for it and now she thinks she's got a pair and — "

"Never mind that," groaned Boots. "They did the same thing with her shotgun. Wilbur opened up another cash on the other side, and some lady just gave him thirty-five bucks for it!"

Bruno held his head and watched as Mr. Sturgeon's blue Plymouth inched its way up the crowded driveway.

"William, calm down," said Mrs. Sturgeon soothingly.

"I am calm," insisted the Headmaster as he finally found a place to park. "I shall remain calm until I get my hands on the boys responsible for this — this flea market!"

"William," she argued, "you know they're only doing it for you and the school. I think you should be proud of them."

Mr. Sturgeon said nothing. With his wife right behind him pointing out the virtues of "the boys who worked so hard for all this," he ploughed through the crowd toward the cash table where Bruno Walton was seated. Halfway there, he ran into James R. Snow, chairman of the Board of Directors of Macdonald Hall. Mr. Snow was examining a framed paint-by-numbers painting of a rather cross-eyed dog when he caught sight of Mr. and Mrs. Sturgeon.

"William. Good afternoon, Mildred," Mr. Snow greeted them. "Congratulations. You must be very proud of your boys for putting together this marvellous sale. And to raise money for the school. Such loyalty! Such school spirit!"

The Headmaster's jaw dropped, but he managed to rise to the occasion. "Oh, yes, Jim. Very proud indeed."

"As a matter of fact," Mr. Snow continued, "I've managed to pick up some real bargains." He held up an old brass umbrella stand. "Look at this beautiful antique for only three dollars."

Mr. Sturgeon feigned a smile. "Lovely, Jim. Just lovely. It seems that you *are* doing well." He turned to his wife. "Mildred, shall we browse?"

Mrs. Sturgeon followed her husband through the crowd toward some of the display tables. When they were out of Mr. Snow's hearing, the Headmaster addressed his wife. "Mildred, that umbrella holder was a wedding present from my great-aunt Agatha."

"Yes, dear, I know that," she replied. "And I've always hated it. But did you hear what Jim Snow said about the sale? He's always so quick to understand the essential points, isn't he, dear?"

Mr. Sturgeon did not reply because he was busy watching Bruno close another deal with Miss Scrimmage. She was buying his favourite old chair, the one he used in his basement retreat. He glared at his wife. His mouth opened and closed several times, but no sound came out. Mrs. Sturgeon just continued smiling.

Having managed to lose his wife in the crowd, at last

Mr. Sturgeon came face to face with Bruno Walton. "I trust business is going well," he said, not without some sarcasm.

"Hello, sir," Bruno greeted him heartily. "I'm glad you could make it. We're really doing great! We'll have enough money for a pool in no time!"

"May I ask what your business hours are?" Mr. Sturgeon consulted his watch. "It's only an hour until dinner. When does the sale end?"

"When we've sold everything, of course," Bruno replied cheerfully. "Everything must go. That's our motto."

"Well, Walton, you have fifteen minutes in which to reach that goal. After that I want everything and everybody off this lawn. The sale is over."

"Yes, sir," said Bruno, much subdued.

"Also," the Headmaster went on, "I would like to see you and O'Neal in my office this evening at half past seven. Please be punctual." And Mr. Sturgeon walked off into the crowd in search of his wife.

Bruno stood up on the sales table and cupped his hands to his mouth. "Fifteen minutes!" he roared. "Fifteen more minutes of fabulous bargains! Fifteen minutes to closing!"

Across the way, he heard the foghorn voice of Wilbur Hackenschleimer taking up the cry. In a little while the campus was cleared.

* * *

"$713.15," Bruno Walton reported to the fund-raising committee at dinner that evening. He indicated four large buckets on the floor under the table. "It's all in there. Boots and I just finished counting it."

"The amount in our possession," announced Elmer Drimsdale, "is 2.8526% of the required amount for the swimming pool, leaving $24,286.85 still to be collected."

The boys were stunned into momentary silence. For a split second even Wilbur paused in his systematic eating.

"I guess it's a whole lot of money," Mark Davies commented, "but I sure expected more."

The boys all murmured their agreement.

Bruno nodded sadly. "I thought we'd make thousands," he agreed. "But anyway, it's a start. And at least Boots and I have something to give to The Fish when we go to his office tonight."

Boots choked on his milk. "The Fish? His office? Tonight?"

"Didn't I mention it?" Bruno asked innocently. "The Fish wants to see us tonight at seven-thirty."

"Well, I don't want to see him," Boots moaned. "We're in trouble again."

"Not to worry," Bruno promised. "We'll dazzle him with our flawless logic and our buckets full of money."

"I know about the money," said Boots, "but would you like to let me in on the logic?"

"Certainly," Bruno replied. "Logic dictates that if

anything threatens the sanctity of Macdonald Hall the threat must be eliminated. Besides, The Fish wants a pool too — he said so."

"And he'll be thrilled with our $713," Boots said sarcastically.

"And fifteen cents," Bruno added. "Yes, he will, because there's plenty more where that came from."

Chris Talbot got up and left the table. "I think I may be sick," he said.

Bruno looked at his watch. "It's quarter after seven. Let's go."

Grabbing two buckets each, he and Boots headed toward the Faculty Building.

Mrs. Davis was out, but the office door was open, allowing Mr. Sturgeon to watch their arrival. "Come in, come in," he said impatiently, ushering them in and seating them on the hard wooden bench they had occupied so many times before. His eyes fell on the four money buckets, and a smile tugged at the corner of his thin mouth. But his expression remained severe.

Bruno spoke up bravely. "We brought you $713.15, sir. The entire proceeds of the sale."

Mr. Sturgeon reached into one of the buckets and removed a ten-dollar bill. "$703.15," he amended. "This is a refund for one of your customers. I had a telephone call a few moments ago from Miss Scrimmage."

"Oh," said Bruno. "You must mean the lamp."

"I do indeed," said the Headmaster sternly. "Did you take it?"

Bruno hesitated. He didn't want to cause trouble for Cathy and Diane. "Uh — I guess we did, sir."

"Indirectly," Boots added.

Mr. Sturgeon seemed to understand. "Then after the ten dollars is refunded, we can safely leave the problem to Miss Scrimmage. Now we come to our problem — or should I say *your* problem?"

The boys remained silent.

"I am still Headmaster of this institution," he went on. "When there are examinations, I know about them. When there are misdemeanors, I attend to them. When the grass is cut, I am consulted. You boys have been at Macdonald Hall long enough to know that nothing — absolutely nothing — is allowed to take place on this campus without my permission. What do you have to say for yourselves?"

"We thought it would be a happy surprise for you, sir," said Bruno meekly, "when you found out we were raising money for the pool."

Mr. Sturgeon nodded. "I realize you meant well," he said, a little less severely. "And that is why I am not going to punish you. But I would like to point out that a great deal of the harm in this world is caused by people with good intentions. There will be no more flea markets."

"Does that mean no more fund-raising, sir?" Bruno

asked anxiously. "We're saving for the pool and we're a little bit short."

Mr. Sturgeon coughed and tried to look grim. But he seemed to hear Mr. Snow's voice: "What school spirit!" and Mildred's: "Oh, William, what harm can it do?" He could not find it in his heart to discourage them.

"You may proceed if you don't get carried away," he said finally.

"Yes, sir," Bruno exclaimed happily.

"And thank you, sir," Boots added.

"Meanwhile," Mr. Sturgeon went on, "I'll keep this money in the office safe for you. I don't like the idea of keeping it in pails in the dormitories. At the earliest opportunity I shall take you boys to the bank and help you open an account for your pool fund. You are dismissed. Good evening."

Bruno and Boots politely smiled their way out of the office. As they left the Faculty Building they met Boots's former roommate, George Wexford-Smyth III, who was nobody's friend and preferred it that way. He was taking his evening constitutional to clear his sinuses.

"Ah," George sneered unpleasantly, "I should have known you two were responsible for that vulgar fish market that took place on campus today. I hope you were properly chastised."

"Watch it, George," Bruno smiled sweetly. "Your blood pressure."

"Goodbye, George," Boots announced firmly. They

walked away and left him.

Bruno smiled happily. "Let's go home," he said with satisfaction. "You're going to write a letter to your folks telling them all about our new pool."

* * *

Mr. Sturgeon hung up his toothbrush, turned off the bathroom light and walked into his darkened bedroom.

Bang!

"Who put that chair there? Mildred, where's my night light?"

"Some passing tourists from California bought it," she said mildly. "And I found that chair at the rummage sale. It was a real buy at eight dollars."

"It probably belonged to the barracuda from across the road," Mr. Sturgeon muttered.

"Now, dear, that's no way to talk about Miss Scrimmage."

He inched his way across the room until his hand touched his night table. There was a large metal box sitting exactly where he always placed his glasses. He picked the box up to move it. There was a sudden snap. Something soft and springy struck him in the face and a recorded voice said, "Hi there! My name is Jack!"

Mr. Sturgeon made no sound. He sat on the edge of the bed until the pounding of his heart returned to normal.

"I bought the jack-in-the-box at the sale too," his wife explained. "I thought it was cute."

"Oh, it *is* cute," he replied calmly. "Very cute."

They were about to settle down to sleep when they heard the police sirens.

Just one of those things

"Scrimmage's is crawling with cops!" Boots exclaimed from his vantage point halfway out the window. "I told you I heard sirens!"

Bruno made no reply, but a familiar fiendish grin spread across his face. "Let's go!" he cried, throwing on his bathrobe. He tore out the door into the corridor, with Boots right behind him. As they ran, they banged on every door. "Red alert! Scrimmage's is being raided!"

Before long, all of Dormitory 3 was milling around in confusion on the dark campus.

"What's going on?"

"Miss Scrimmage got busted!"

"The girls are in danger!"

"Bunny rabbit slippers, Fred?"

"Who woke me up?"

"I never did trust Miss Scrimmage! She has small eyes!"

The growing din woke up the other two dormitories, and in a matter of minutes the entire population of Macdonald Hall was howling and surging across the road and onto the grounds of Miss Scrimmage's Finishing School for Young Ladies. Girls in pink nighties fluttered out to meet them.

Cathy Burton's voice boomed over the school's public address system: *Our beloved leader is falsely accused! Save Miss Scrimmage!*

At the very instant that Bruno and Boots arrived on the scene, Miss Scrimmage was being escorted out the front door by two extremely large police officers. The crowd went wild, blocking their passage.

Diane Grant ran up to Bruno and spun him around. "Bruno, you've got to do something!"

"All right. I'll bake her a cake with a file in it."

"Bruno, this isn't funny!" Diane exclaimed, quite upset. "It's all your fault anyway!"

"My fault?" Bruno repeated.

"His fault?" Boots echoed.

Cathy's high-pitched voice came over the speaker again: *Don't forget, Miss Scrimmage, you have the right to remain silent!*

A desperate-looking policeman shouted to his partner, "Barney, where the heck did all these kids come from?"

"I don't know," Barney called back, "but stay away from the girls. They kick! Ouch! They scratch too!"

"Do something!" Diane screeched. "Cathy! Cathy!"

Cathy Burton burst out onto Miss Scrimmage's balcony and screamed, "All right, girls! Lie down in front of the cars!"

Amid cheers from the students of both schools, the girls flopped down on the ground all around the police cars.

"We demand to hear the charges!" Cathy screamed again.

One of the officers held up both hands for order and replied in a loud voice that could be heard by all, "The charge is armed robbery!"

Silence fell like a stone. Even Bruno Walton was unable to react with anything but mute astonishment. A full sixty seconds went by, and then the crowd began to murmur.

"Armed robbery?"

"Miss *Scrimmage?*"

"I knew it! Small eyes will tell!"

"I wonder where she stashed the loot."

"She'll get twenty years for this!"

"Maybe she's innocent!"

"People with small eyes are *never* innocent!"

Suddenly a quiet voice penetrated the din. "I will have order!" Again the crowd fell silent. Even the policemen came to attention. Mr. Sturgeon, in his red silk bathrobe and bedroom slippers, had arrived on the scene.

"Oh, Mr. Sturgeon, thank heaven you're here!"

shrilled Miss Scrimmage, her hair curlers bobbing in agitation. "Tell them, please tell them that I didn't do it!"

"I'm sure you didn't, Miss Scrimmage," said the Headmaster of Macdonald Hall. "What is it you are supposed to have done?"

"Armed robbery, sir," Bruno announced loudly.

Mr. Sturgeon froze him with his famous steely-grey stare and turned to the police officer who seemed to be in charge. "Armed robbery of what? And when?"

"A couple of hours ago a woman answering her description robbed Joe's Hardware Store on Highway 14," was the reply. "She left this behind." He reached into one of the patrol cars and pulled out a 12-gauge shotgun. "It has the name and address of this place engraved on the stock."

Miss Scrimmage screamed and collapsed into the arms of the two officers who flanked her. The girls began screaming too. Bruno and Boots exchanged a quick look of understanding and moved backwards into the thick of the crowd. In a few seconds they returned, herding the burly form of Wilbur Hackenschleimer ahead of them.

"We sold the shotgun this afternoon, sir," Bruno confessed. "Wilbur can describe the lady who bought it."

"She was tall and skinny and old, sir, just like Miss Scrimmage," Wilbur blurted out, then immediately

clapped his immense hands over his mouth. "I mean
— "

"I know what you mean, Hackenschleimer," said Mr.
Sturgeon. He turned to the police officers. "Gentlemen," he explained, "through some — error, Miss
Scrimmage's shotgun was sold at a rummage sale this
afternoon. In addition, I can attest to Miss Scrimmage's
whereabouts this evening as I was talking to her on the
telephone — several times. Her staff and students will
assure you that she did not leave the residence. This has
been a ghastly mistake."

"Ghastly, ghastly!" moaned Miss Scrimmage who
was just reviving, to the great relief of the two
policemen who had been holding her up.

"Well, then," said one of the officers, "you seem to
have an alibi, ma'am."

"An alibi indeed!" cried the outraged Miss Scrimmage. "Young man, you should be ashamed of yourself,
bursting in here and victimizing a defenceless woman
and terrifying these innocent girls!"

"Lady," said one of the younger officers, "Godzilla
couldn't terrify these girls!"

"Our apologies, ma'am," continued the policeman in
charge. "It was unfortunate, but unavoidable in view of
the evidence." He smiled placatingly. "You must be
very proud of the loyalty shown by your young ladies."

Miss Scrimmage shook herself like a hen resetting
her ruffled feathers. "Well, I suppose it couldn't be

helped," she said at last. "I shall attempt to forget it. May I please have my shotgun?"

"No, ma'am, not yet. It was used in a robbery and we need it for evidence."

Miss Scrimmage was alarmed. "How can you leave us defenceless? I need that shotgun to protect my girls!"

"Lady," laughed the same young officer, limping towards his car, "I pity the poor sucker who tries to break into *this* place!"

As the last of the police cars pulled out of Miss Scrimmage's driveway, Mr. Sturgeon addressed his students. "Classes will be delayed one hour in the morning" — he stared down a few weak cheers — "and extended one extra hour into the afternoon. You will all return to your beds immediately."

* * *

Bruno smothered his laughter with his pillow to avoid disturbing the House Master.

"I don't see what's so funny," said Boots. "Tomorrow The Fish is going to kill us for this."

"Oh, he will not," scoffed Bruno. "How many times can he bawl us out for the same thing? The Fish knows as well as we do that the girls took the shotgun, the same as they took the lamp. Stop worrying. You're beginning to get on my nerves."

"You don't have any nerves," Boots accused him.

"How could you stand up in front of everybody and holler 'armed robbery' at Miss Scrimmage?"

"Well, somebody had to do it," Bruno laughed. "Boots, where's your sense of humour? Don't you realize they were hauling her off to the slammer?"

Boots smiled a little in the darkness. "I'd find it funnier if I wasn't sure it was all our fault."

"It wasn't anybody's fault," Bruno assured him. "It was just one of those things that seem to happen a lot around here. Besides, it was one of our better riots."

Boots yawned. "On our scale of one to ten, it was at least a nine," he agreed. "I'm tired."

"Mmmm," Bruno grunted. "We'll need a good night's sleep. We've got a lot of work to do on the talent show."

There was dead silence from the other bed. Then, "What talent show?" Boots demanded suspiciously.

But Bruno had already begun to snore.

* * *

"Oh, Mildred, you should have seen it!" exclaimed Mr. Sturgeon as he climbed into bed for the second time that night. "Children all over the place, and the police dragging the barracuda off to jail!"

"William, I've asked you not to use that name. Poor Miss Scrimmage! What a horrible ordeal for her."

"We haven't heard the end of this," her husband

chuckled sleepily. "I should have let them take her away."

"William, how can you talk that way?"

He laughed again. "It wouldn't have done me any good. Before they locked her up they would have allowed her one telephone call. She probably would have called me!"

Ring!

In the dark, Mr. Sturgeon fumbled for the telephone on his night table. His elbow struck something as he lifted the receiver. Before he could speak, a recorded voice said, "Hi there! My name is Jack!"

"Hello? . . . No, Miss Scrimmage, you do not have the wrong number . . . Don't mention it, Miss Scrimmage. You're quite welcome. Any time . . . Oh, yes. I quite agree. Heaven forbid . . . Why, Miss Scrimmage, how dare you accuse my boys of stealing your shotgun? . . . Your young ladies, that's who . . . No, Miss Scrimmage, I do not wish to wager . . . I most certainly do not intend to punish anyone . . . Oh, I'm running a zoo, am I? Well, it's *your* school that has all the wild animals. Goodnight!"

Mr. Sturgeon hung up forcefully. "Mildred, that woman is going to drive me crazy!"

"Now, dear . . ."

Impresario at work

Mr. Sturgeon stepped away from the teller's cage, followed by Bruno and Boots. The Headmaster handed Bruno a new, gold-coloured bankbook.

"Here it is," he said. "$703.15, registered to your signatures in trust for Macdonald Hall. It is a great responsibility, and I hope you will look after it with care."

"Of course, sir," promised Boots.

The three left the bank and climbed into the Headmaster's blue Plymouth for the trip back to school.

"Sir," Bruno announced as they got under way, "we have another great plan for raising money."

Mr. Sturgeon's knuckles whitened on the steering wheel. "I suspected it wouldn't take you very long," he remarked grimly. "Would you be so good as to outline the nature of this plan, and I shall determine whether or not it is great."

"It's a talent show, sir," said Bruno eagerly. "We'll

audition anyone who wants to try out."

"And the tickets will be a dollar apiece," Boots added.

Mr. Sturgeon examined the proposal from every possible angle. It *seemed* harmless enough, even though it came from Bruno and Boots.

"I think I might give permission for that," he said grudgingly. "Perhaps the parents would like to be invited."

"At five bucks a head," Bruno added with growing enthusiasm.

"Walton," Mr. Sturgeon said gently, "if the parents take the time and expense to attend this affair, they should be admitted at the going rate."

Visions of dollar signs vanished from Bruno's imagination. "Right, sir," he agreed sadly.

"Do you think maybe, sir, we could combine with Miss Scrimmage's school for the show?" Boots ventured timidly.

"That's a swell idea!" exclaimed Bruno, who had put his roommate up to suggesting it in the first place. "The more people, the more talent!" Both boys eyed their Headmaster expectantly.

Mr. Sturgeon was silent. Memories of his last telephone conversation with Miss Scrimmage danced crazily through his mind. She was probably still angry and would doubtless refuse to allow her school to participate. Holding that hope, he said, "Very well. I shall take it up with Miss Scrimmage."

"Then we have your permission to begin auditions?" Bruno asked excitedly.

Mr. Sturgeon nodded a wary nod.

* * *

The door of room 107, Chris Talbot's room, burst open and in barged Bruno and Boots, unannounced and uninvited. In the centre of the room stood Chris, wrapped in a towel. His roommate, a freshman, cowered in terror at his desk.

"Don't worry," Chris assured him kindly. "They're harmless. They just never learned to knock." He greeted the intruders with an elaborate sweep of his hand. "Don't be shy. Come right in."

Bruno flopped down on the nearest bed and sniffed the air. "What stinks in here?" he asked, wrinkling his nose.

"It isn't in here," Chris explained patiently. "That lunatic next door is disinfecting his room."

"Sterilizing," Boots corrected. "That's George Wexford-Smyth III, my old roommate. He does this every forty-eight hours."

"He must use a lot of spray," said the freshman. "It sure smells strong."

"Oh, George won't use aerosol propellant — not since the warnings were published. If he destroys the ozone layer," Boots explained, "the ultra-violet rays from the sun will get him. He doesn't spray the room. He washes it. *All* of it."

"Mr. Clean," Bruno commented. "Chris, do you have a little spare time?"

"Well, I was thinking of doing my homework and —"

"Oh, that. Well, this is important," Bruno interrupted. "We need eight posters advertising the auditions for our talent show."

Chris reached for pen and paper. "The details," he said, all business.

* * *

"I think the talent show is a wonderful idea," said Mrs. Sturgeon that evening as she counted out the Monopoly money for their weekly game.

"I couldn't agree more," said Miss Scrimmage from across the table. "My girls are very enthusiastic. They're making their costumes in sewing class."

"How delightful," responded Mr. Sturgeon, who hated Monopoly except that it eliminated the necessity for polite conversation during Miss Scrimmage's weekly visits. "Shall we begin? You are first, Miss Scrimmage."

Miss Scrimmage gave the dice an enthusiastic toss, and the number came up seven. She advanced her token seven spaces, reached for a Chance card, and read: *"Go to jail, go directly to . . . "* Her voice trailed off.

The sound that escaped Mr. Sturgeon was suspiciously like a snicker. Under the table, his wife kicked him sharply. As he picked up the dice, he decided he did not dislike Monopoly so much after all.

* * *

The next day, little was accomplished during the last class of the afternoon, as the suddenly stage-struck student body watched the clock. Auditions for the talent show were scheduled to begin at four o'clock sharp.

In his Canadian history class, Bruno Walton dropped an ever-so-subtle hint to the teacher. "Three-thirty already?" he mused loudly. "My, how time flies."

"Very well, that will be all for today," the teacher decided. "We can't have the impresario being late for his auditions. Dismissed."

Bruno met Boots in the hallway, and the two boys dashed off towards the school auditorium. A stampede of undiscovered stars followed along behind them. They were met by a surging crowd of girls from Miss Scrimmage's.

"Okay!" Bruno bellowed to quiet down the crowd. "Come in and sit down. We'll start right away. We require complete silence. Everybody has to have a fair chance to compete. Boots, bring on the first act."

Boots produced the registration lists that had been attached to Chris Talbot's posters. "The first act is Percy the Great," he announced.

One of the first-year boys appeared, lugging a large sheet of plywood. Attached to the wood was a department store dummy with a grotesque smile. In his belt the boy carried four sharp knives.

"A knife thrower?" Bruno asked incredulously.

"Yes," said Percy the Great. "Naturally when I do the show it will be with a live volunteer from the audience instead of a dummy."

"Naturally," said Bruno. "Go ahead. Let's see what you can do."

Obediently, Percy the Great danced around the stage, flourishing a razor-sharp knife. At last he held it gracefully by the tip, reared back and let fly.

Snap! The knife neatly severed the dummy's head at the neck. The still smiling head rolled across the stage and came to rest at Bruno's feet.

When the laughter and cheers died down, Bruno said firmly, "Sorry, Percy, old boy, but your real live volunteer is going to end up real dead. Next act."

"Elmer Drimsdale," Boots announced dubiously.

Elmer ascended the stage and looked hopefully at Bruno through his thick glasses.

"What do you do, Elm?" Bruno asked in surprise. Elmer was known as a genius, but no one was aware that he had any talent.

"My act," he said timidly, "is entitled 'The Song of the Hump-Backed Whale.' "

Everyone tittered except Bruno Walton, who had once roomed with Elmer and half expected something of the sort.

"Go ahead. Let's hear it."

Screwing his face up horribly, Elmer emitted a series of grunts, groans, mournful moans, squeals and moos. Finally, his face and voice back to normal, he explained, "Whales converse in this way. That was symbolic of 'Greetings' or perhaps 'A whale is here.' "

Bruno observed the audience reaction, which ranged from broad smiles to howls of hysteria. He signalled for order and got it.

"Elmer, that was great! But it was too short."

"I also do bird calls," Elmer offered hopefully.

Bruno slammed a fist into his palm with delight. "I don't even have to hear them! You work on it and be ready for rehearsal. You're in the show. Boots, put down Elmer Drimsdale."

"As what?" Boots asked.

"As a — an impressionist of nature," Bruno declared. "Next act."

Next was a pair of seniors from Macdonald Hall who had brought along their own record, straw hats and canes, and shuffled around the stage, bumping into each other, roughly in time to the music. They promised faithfully to polish up the act with practice, and Boots put them down as a possibility.

"Next."

"Eleanor Noseworthy," Boots called out.

A short plump girl appeared on the stage. "I do a gourmet act," she informed them proudly.

"Great," said Bruno. "Uh — what exactly is that?"

"I prepare a dish that I call 'Boeuf Noseworthy avec Oignons.' "

"Uh — " Bruno stammered, "we have no facilities for cooking on stage. Sorry. Next act."

"The Amazing Frederick," Boots announced.

The curtains parted to reveal the Amazing Frederick himself, carrying a large fishtank filled with water.

"Well, what's your act?" asked Bruno, somewhat wearily.

"I hold my head under water for three minutes," replied the Amazing Frederick.

"All right," Bruno said. "Go to it."

Everyone watched with awe as the Amazing Frederick drew an enormous breath and plunged his head into the fishtank, his face towards the audience.

Two minutes passed in total silence. Then the crowd began to get edgy as the Amazing Frederick's contorted face went from red to purple to blue and the bubbles started rising.

"Bruno, pull him out! He's drowning!"

"He'll die!"

"He's my brother! *Leave him there!*"

"Help!"

Around the three minute mark, the Amazing Frederick heaved himself out of the tank, drew another mighty breath, wrapped his head in a large beach towel and collapsed, amid thunderous applause from all present.

"Boots," called Bruno, "sign him up. He'll be a smash!"

Shaking his head in a what-will-they-think-of-next manner, Boots put the Amazing Frederick down on his list.

Bruno then proceeded to turn down a singer who must have attracted every dog within hearing range of Macdonald Hall, a tap dancer who was fair until she slipped and twisted her ankle, a barbershop quartet who accomplished about as much harmony as a diesel horn, and two comedy skits that weren't funny at all.

"Next," Bruno said. He was becoming bored.

"The — Scrimmettes?"

Cathy Burton climbed onto the stage and whispered to Bruno at great length.

"Put the Scrimmettes down for the show, Boots," called Bruno as Cathy left the stage. "Next."

"Super Hackenschleimer," announced Boots, who

was no longer surprised by anything.

This was, of course, Wilbur Hackenschleimer, who pledged that he would lift a piano for the show. Bruno was thrilled with the idea, though the crowd had other reactions.

"Don't let him do it, Bruno!"

"He'll wind up in traction!"

"He'll kill himself!"

"A hernia!"

"A slipped disc!"

"Why would anybody want to lift a piano?"

But Bruno's decision was final, and Super Hackenschleimer was in show business.

"Next."

Next was a magician who wasn't too bad at demonstrating that the hand was quicker than the eye — if not *his* hand. He promised to polish his routine, though, and Bruno had Boots sign him up because the show needed a magic act.

The auditions went on until five-thirty when the dinner bell rang. While en route to the dining hall, Bruno and Boots discussed the acts they had seen, and which of the "possibles" deserved to be put into the show. It was in the cafeteria line that they found themselves standing next to George Wexford-Smyth III.

"What outrageous sort of contest were you organizing in the auditorium today?" George asked Bruno in disgust. "It caused a stampede in the hall and I was almost trampled!"

"It's not for you," Boots cut in. "It's vulgar."

"I would expect it to be," said George as Bruno and Boots abandoned him and took their trays off to their table.

*　*　*

Tickets for the big show, scheduled for a week from Saturday, went on sale immediately. Invitations were mailed out to the parents, and quite a few agreed to attend. Rehearsals began in earnest.

Bruno had appointed himself Master of Ceremonies, and in addition to running the rehearsals, he and Boots were hard at work putting together short comedy routines to spot in between the various acts. Late one night, after lights-out, Bruno hauled Boots out of bed with an idea for yet another hilarious skit.

"I finally get to sleep after writing one of those ridiculous letters to my parents about how happy I am at the Hall — the fourth one in two days!" Boots moaned, " — and you have to wake me up! Why can't you get your ideas in the daytime?"

"Because in the daytime my head is all balled up with math and geography and junk like that. Now, listen. You'll come out and say: 'Good evening, ladies and germs.' "

"Are you crazy?" Boots exploded. "People stopped laughing at that fifty years ago!"

"Comedy doesn't change," Bruno lectured him. "If it was funny fifty years ago, it'll be funny in our show."

"We'll be lynched," Boots predicted mournfully. "That's even worse than your 'ugliest man in the world' routine."

"Oh, go back to bed!" Bruno grumbled. "You have the sense of humour of a loaf of bread! You'll be happier at York Academy where nobody laughs because they're too stupid!"

"And what about some of the acts?" Boots continued. "What about Wilbur? He doesn't come to rehearsal. How do we know he can lift a piano?"

"Don't worry. Wilbur could lift the auditorium and everybody in it."

"What about the Scrimmettes?" Boots persisted. "We haven't even seen their act!"

"They're rehearsing privately," said Bruno.

"That's Cathy, Bruno! *Cathy!* There's no telling what they'll do!"

"They dance," Bruno replied calmly. "They have all kinds of ballet lessons at Scrimmage's. I'm sure they'll be good."

They were interrupted by a tapping at the door and

the voice of the House Master, Mr. Fudge. "Hey, knock it off in there. It's past midnight."

Bruno and Boots went back to bed.

On stage, please

"Boots, we're playing to a full house!" exclaimed Bruno as he peeked through the curtains.

"I saw," replied Boots, trying to ignore the nervous quivering of his stomach. "Bruno, do we really have to do all that stupid stuff, especially 'the ugliest man in the world'?"

"We do the show *as is,*" Bruno insisted. "We'll be great." He turned as Diane Grant rushed up, all a-twitter. "What's the matter?"

"Bruno," she said breathlessly, "Cathy says we have to have a pair of large scissors or our act is ruined!"

"Boots, get a pair of scissors for the Scrimmettes." Bruno walked away to check on his other acts, reflecting that the life of a stage manager wasn't too hard after all.

A last-minute addition to the cast was Perry Elbert, a gymnast. He shrank back at Bruno's approach. "No offense, Bruno, but please go away. In the past our relationship has been a hazardous one — for me, that is."

"Really?" Bruno said in surprise. "What have I done?"

"Nothing actually," sighed Perry. "You give me a chocolate bar and I lose a filling in it. You help me with my suitcase and the lock disintegrates so I have to pick up clothes for half an hour — that kind of thing. Things just happen to me when you're around. I'll probably break my neck out there!"

"You're going to be great," Bruno soothed him. "Five minutes, everybody. Five minutes."

Bruno made a last-minute check of the lighting crew and the boy who was operating the record player. Everything was ready. The time had arrived. The house lights dimmed, the music started and Bruno Walton, clad in his best suit and a large bow tie, stepped out into the spotlight. The applause was deafening. Bruno was delighted — he hadn't even done anything yet, and he was already a success!

Click! A camera flash momentarily blinded him. When the green spots faded from his eyes, he recognized Mrs. Sturgeon, waving her camera and smiling encouragement at him from the front row.

"Good evening, ladies and gentlemen, and welcome to the first annual Macdonald Hall-Miss Scrimmage's Talent Show. Proceeds will go towards our swimming pool fund. We have a great variety show planned, starring students from both schools and featuring as our *pièce de résistance,* the world première performance of the Scrimmettes."

In his front row seat, Mr. Sturgeon winced. Beside him, Miss Scrimmage beamed.

"So let's swing into our first act," Bruno went on enthusiastically, "a dance team with four left feet. Ha, ha, little joke there. Our soft-shoe dancers, Hughie and Louie!"

Bruno scrambled off stage, and the curtains parted on Hughie and Louie. For the first sixty seconds or so, Hughie and Louie were doing quite well. But then Mrs. Sturgeon leaped up and again her camera flashed, blinding Hughie, who turned the wrong way and rammed face-first into Louie. They never quite got back on track after that, but nevertheless they received deafening applause when they finally stumbled to a finish.

Bruno reappeared, applauding wildly. "Weren't they great, folks? And this is only the beginning. There's plenty of talent to come, so please don't walk out on us. Ha, ha, another little joke."

He beamed and continued. "You know, because this is a school project, we wanted to use something in our show that would demonstrate how concerned we are about our environment. And here to show us all what our environment sounds like is our impressionist of nature, Elmer Drimsdale!"

Stricken by stage-fright, Elmer walked out onto the platform like a wind-up toy. Once there, spurred on by the applause, he took a deep breath and launched into his imitation of a hump-backed whale, forgetting the introduction he had planned. The spectacle of a skinny, crew-cut boy making faces and mooing at them without explanation shocked the audience into awed silence. When Elmer finished, there wasn't a sound.

"The words, Elmer! The words!" Bruno whispered frantically. Everyone in the house heard him except Elmer who, now really into his act, had begun to chirp lustily. The audience was more at home with these sounds, recognizing the bird calls for what they were. Backstage, Bruno Walton was tearing his hair and laughing. But out in the spotlight, Elmer was in his glory, chirping, twittering and tweeting. Finally he fell silent and surveyed the stunned audience.

"Are there any questions?"

One of the parents stood up. "I recognized all your bird calls except the first one," he said. "What was that first call you did?"

Elmer looked thoroughly bewildered. "That wasn't a bird call," he said. "That was the song of the hump-backed whale, of course."

The audience erupted into laughter, cheers and applause.

Elmer was ecstatic. "Are there any requests?"

"Can you do the mating call of the great horned

owl?" asked the science teacher from Miss Scrimmage's.

"Certainly," Elmer replied. He folded his hands, closed his eyes, rounded his mouth and began to hoot madly.

A large bundle of brown feathers shot in through the open window of the skylight, headed for the stage and began circling over Elmer, flying slower and slower until it became apparent to everyone that Elmer's life-like imitation had attracted a great horned owl in search of a mate. It was unfortunate that Miss Scrimmage wore a hat lavishly trimmed with brown feathers. The bird, spying the love of its life, hooted happily and began its romantic approach.

"Hit the deck!" bellowed Bruno from the edge of the curtain.

Miss Scrimmage screamed as the bird swooped down, snatching the hat from her head. With one great flap of its powerful wings, it soared to the top of the building and out through the window, hat and all. Immediately two stage hands scrambled up onto the ledge and heaved at the pulley to shut the window.

The audience went wild. Some of the students were standing on their chairs screaming. Mr. Sturgeon was down on the floor trying to revive Miss Scrimmage by fanning her with his handkerchief. Elmer, who had noticed nothing out of the ordinary, was bowing, waving and smiling in triumphant response to his standing ovation.

Bruno was also out on stage, trying to calm everybody down. "Elmer Drimsdale, ladies and gentlemen. Wasn't that some act? Not quite what you expected, was it?"

It was some time before people were back in their seats and the show could go on.

Next on the agenda was the first of the comedy routines created by Bruno and so dreaded by Boots. While Bruno was indulging in easy patter with the audience about the superb quality of the acts to come, Boots crept onto the stage on all fours, studying the floor intently. Bruno pretended not to notice him until Boots bumped into his leg.

Bruno: *(looking down in disgust)* What are you
            doing out here? Can't you see I'm trying to
            do a show?

Boots: *(still studying floor)* I'm looking for my
            contact lens. I lost it backstage.

Bruno: Well, if you lost it backstage, why are you
            looking for it out here?

Boots: Because the light is better out here.

Boots crept off stage amid polite applause from the adults and cheers and jeers from the students.

"Moving right along," Bruno continued brightly, "we have our lovely singer, Janet Black, who will sing 'This Land is Your Land,' accompanying herself on the ukelele." Leaving the stage to the singer, he stepped into the wings where an angry Boots was waiting.

"Bruno, I am *not* going to make a fool of myself again! That was bad enough, but the other one is 'the ugliest man in the world,' and I just can't stand it!"

"Haven't you got ears?" Bruno exclaimed. "They loved it! The whole show's going over great!"

"But Bruno — "

"I'll take complaints tomorrow," Bruno told him.

On stage, Janet Black was doing well. The audience was singing and clapping along with her, and when Mrs. Sturgeon snapped her picture, she didn't even flinch. The song ended to thunderous applause.

Next was the death-defying act of the Amazing Frederick. It was a show-stopper. Mr. Sturgeon fidgeted in his chair as he watched one of his students, to all intents and purposes, drowning himself. Finally, at about the two-and-a-half-minute mark in the submersion, a woman in the seventh row leaped to her feet and began screaming.

"My baby! Freddie, stop it this instant!"

Miss Scrimmage was quick to join the mother's wailing.

By the time the Amazing Frederick, apparently still alive and well, had collapsed on the stage with his chest heaving and his head in a towel, the audience was in a frenzy.

Bruno grasped the microphone. "The Amazing

Frederick, folks, and wasn't he wonderful?"

The mother cried, "Wait till I get my hands on you, Freddie!" sending the audience into gales of laughter.

"And now, ladies and gentlemen, we take pride in presenting our super-gymnast — Perry Elbert!"

Perry cartwheeled onto the stage and began a series of leaps, bounds, somersaults, headstands, stretches and bends, all to music. He was a real trouper, getting through the flash of Mrs. Sturgeon's camera and even ignoring the three times his record became stuck.

While he was taking his bows after a flawless performance, Perry was thinking happily that the jinx was broken. Bruno hadn't gotten to him this time. Then Bruno bounded onto the stage shouting, "That was great!" He awarded Perry a mighty slap on the back and Perry went sprawling off the stage head-first, into the lap of Mr. Sturgeon. Both he and the Headmaster ended up on the floor.

Perry scrambled up and shot Bruno an accusing glance before turning to assist Mr. Sturgeon. Fortunately the Headmaster was unhurt.

On stage, Bruno carried on. "I draw your attention, ladies and gentlemen, to the spotlight at the centre of our stage." The spotlight was focused on the huge grand piano. Underneath the piano squatted Wilbur Hackenschleimer. "Introducing Super Hackenschleimer who will, before your very eyes, lift this immensely colossal piano. May I have a drum roll please."

There was the sound of a needle scratching on a record and the drum roll started. Slowly, Wilbur began to stand up. Sweat poured down his face, and terrible grunts and groans burst from him. With agonizing slowness, his shoulders lifted the piano as he straightened his legs.

Mr. Sturgeon put an iron grip on his wife's camera. "Mildred, don't you dare flash that thing in the boy's face!" he whispered tensely. "He'll drop our piano — our *only* piano!"

The piano teetered dangerously on Wilbur's immense shoulders, as he stood upright. The audience broke into a thunderous ovation. Mr. Sturgeon held his breath while the Macdonald Hall strongman eased himself back onto his knees and let the piano safely down onto the floor. Then and only then did Mrs. Sturgeon stand up and snap a picture of Super Hackenschleimer panting and flexing his muscles in victory.

"Well, what do you know!" exclaimed Boots O'Neal to himself in the wings. "He *can* lift a piano!"

His feeling of elation was instantly replaced by profound embarrassment. Wilbur's act was finished, and that meant it was time for 'the ugliest man in the world' routine. Boots would have given a great deal to avoid it, but he pictured himself at York Academy and knew he couldn't let Bruno down. Not now.

"And now, ladies and gentlemen, a special treat," he heard Bruno say. "The famous Melvin P. O'Neal of

Macdonald Hall — who plans to *stay* at Macdonald Hall — has searched the world over and found the person who is, without question, the ugliest man in the world. Bring him out, Mr. O'Neal."

Boots appeared, leading one of the stage hands who had a towel draped over his head.

"Is this the ugliest man in the world?" Bruno asked.

Boots nodded miserably.

"Are you going to allow anyone to look at the ugliest man in the world?"

Again Boots nodded miserably.

Hughie, one of the soft-shoe dancers, approached the ugliest man in the world, peeked under the towel, cried out in horror and fell to the stage in a dead faint.

Next Cathy Burton marched out, wearing a full-length raincoat. She lifted the towel, let out a shriek that raised the audience out of their seats, and collapsed beside Hughie.

"What's all this?" Bruno exclaimed. "He can't be that bad. I'll have to see for myself."

Bruno walked over as the others had done, lifted the towel and peeked inside. The ugliest man in the world screamed and fainted.

Waves of laughter and applause rolled across the audience and reached the stage.

Boots was astounded. "I thought it was going to be terrible!" he blurted out, right into the microphone. "They're laughing! You may be a genius after all!"

The laughter doubled as Boots's exclamation was carried throughout the auditorium. The dreaded 'ugliest man in the world' routine was a smash hit.

"There's a lot more to come," Bruno announced when order was restored, "including the drawing for our door prize and, finally, the fabulous Scrimmettes. But first we'll have a fifteen minute intermission. Don't go away." And the curtain closed to engulf him.

Down the aisles rolled the dining room tea wagons, manned by students who were chanting: "Ice cold orangeade, ten cents! Get your fresh and delicious Scrim-cakes here! Fifteen cents!"

The idea of selling drinks and cupcakes at intermission had come from Wilbur Hackenschleimer, who had been unable to imagine anyone sitting through an entire performance without food. Bruno had charmed the orangeade out of the Macdonald Hall kitchen staff. The Scrim-cakes had been baked in Miss Scrimmage's cooking class.

Bruno and Boots had been delighted with the idea because it provided another source of revenue. This was the first Mr. Sturgeon had heard of it, however. As he bit into a rather hard cupcake, he reflected that although he had given permission for this talent show, he had been consulted on very little else.

"Aren't these delicious!" Mrs. Sturgeon exclaimed, much to the delight of Miss Scrimmage, who was very proud of the accomplishments of her girls.

Backstage, Bruno was met by a white-faced Boots O'Neal. "Bruno, come quick!" he practically gibbered. "The Scrimmettes! They used the scissors to — "

"Not now," Bruno interrupted. "Intermission is almost over."

"But Bruno, we'll be expelled!"

"Why should we be expelled? The show is great! Where's Sidney? I'm going out to introduce him."

Bruno walked out on stage. "Hello again, ladies and gentlemen. I hope you enjoyed your little snack. Next from our all-star cast we have for you our juggler, Old Butterfingers — ha, ha, little joke there — Sidney Rampulsky!"

Sidney started out with Indian clubs, and after a perfect performance, switched to eggs. He was doing fine with first three and then four eggs until an enraptured Mrs. Sturgeon jumped up and snapped his picture, disrupting his concentration. The eggs flew from his hands and, one by one, as though aimed by an evil spirit, splattered against Miss Scrimmage's face. When the blindness caused by the flashbulb faded from his eyes and he saw what he had done, Sidney Butterfingers Rampulsky turned and ran. The audience lapsed into an embarassed silence.

As usual, it was Bruno who broke the ice. "We can have a few minutes delay," he offered, "in case anyone wants to — uh — go to the bathroom and wash egg-yolk off her face."

Miss Scrimmage rushed up the aisle, followed by a solicitous Mrs. Sturgeon.

The Headmaster beckoned to Bruno. "I don't suppose anyone thought to have those eggs hard-boiled," he said sarcastically.

"Well, no, sir," Bruno replied. "We never thought Butterfingers was going to throw them at anyone."

Mr. Sturgeon grimaced. "I trust there will be no more surprises this evening?"

"Of course not, sir. Everything's going to be fine."

In a few minutes the ladies returned to their seats and Bruno introduced Marie Latousse, virtuoso of the concert piano. Marie, a junior student at Miss Scrimmage's, played the piece she had been rehearsing for two weeks — "Hot Cross Buns." It was very well received, but there could be no encore. "Hot Cross Buns" was the only selection that Marie could play.

"Boy, wasn't she terrific!" Bruno exclaimed. "And wait till you see what we've got for you now! Introducing Marvin the Magnificent, who will dazzle you with his supernatural powers."

Marvin the Magnificent, the magician who had promised to polish up his act, was doing a fine job. He started with a few card tricks, sawed Boots in half and made Bruno disappear.

"I've got to find out how that's done," Mr. Sturgeon whispered to his wife.

"Oh, William!"

"For my last trick," Marvin announced, "I will pull a rabbit out of this totally empty hat." Mrs. Sturgeon readied her camera. Marvin reached into the hat and triumphantly drew out a small white rabbit which he displayed to the audience.

Flash! The rabbit panicked, and using the top of Miss Scrimmage's head as a jumping-off point, headed for the back of the auditorium.

Without hesitation, Mr. Sturgeon whipped out his trusty handkerchief and began to fan the semi-conscious Miss Scrimmage. He eyed Bruno accusingly.

At the back of the hall, two usherettes were luring the rabbit from under a seat, using a left-over Scrim-cake as bait. The terrified animal was soon restored to Marvin, but not before he had paid Bruno fifteen cents for the Scrim-cake.

"And now, ladies and gentlemen," Bruno announced, "get your ticket stubs ready because it's time to draw for our door prize." Boots wheeled onto the stage a tea cart containing a fish bowl full of ticket stubs and a brightly wrapped package. "The prize was donated by our own Mrs. Sturgeon." There was polite applause. "As a reward for locating the ugliest man in the world, I'm going to call upon Mr. Melvin P. O'Neal to draw the winning number."

Boots reached into the bowl, picked a ticket and handed it to Bruno.

"And the winning number is — 119."

There was a murmur as people checked their tickets; then Mrs. Sturgeon's voice rang through the hall. "William, that's *your* number!"

Mr. Sturgeon climbed onto the stage to collect his prize. His wife stood poised, ready to capture the moment on film.

"What a surprise," said Bruno. "Congratulations, sir." He picked up the package and thrust it into Mr. Sturgeon's hands.

There was an all too familiar click. A soft object burst up through the wrapping paper and struck the Headmaster in the face. A recorded voice said, *"Hi there! My name is Jack!"* just as the flashbulb went off. Mr. Sturgeon got a standing ovation as he carried his old nemesis back to his seat.

"And now, ladies and germs — ha, ha, little joke there — the moment you've all been waiting for." Bruno was waxing enthusiastic while, backstage, Boots was holding his head. "We take great pride in presenting — *The Scrimmettes!*"

To the music of a hit Broadway show, the six Scrimmettes danced onto the stage, wearing little more than the smiles on their faces. Miss Scrimmage screamed in horror and slumped back in her seat, unable to take her eyes off the row of shapely legs. Even Bruno was shocked. He suddenly realized what Boots had been trying to tell him — that Cathy had used the scissors to modify the conservative sewing class ballet costumes.

Pandemonium broke loose as the Macdonald Hall boys stood up on their chairs and whistled.

Mr. Sturgeon leaned over to Miss Scrimmage. "You say the girls made these costumes in sewing class?"

Miss Scrimmage was beside herself. "They looked — *larger* when I saw them," she managed to reply. "They had — skirts attached."

Mrs. Sturgeon rose to the occasion. "They're lovely," she said comfortingly. "And the girls are excellent dancers."

That was undeniable. The Scrimmettes were nothing short of sensational. In spite of the fact that they could no longer hear their music over the din, they staged a show that was worthy of the Rockettes of Radio City Music Hall. Their finale of precision high kicks brought the house down. When they left the stage, the cheers were the loudest that had ever been heard in the Macdonald Hall auditorium.

Bruno reappeared at the microphone. "That's our show, ladies and gentlemen. We hope you've enjoyed our talent. Thank you for coming. Goodnight, all."

The final ovation was deafening.

*   *   *

By the light of a flashlight, Bruno and Boots, still

flushed with the success of the talent show, huddled at Boots's desk.

"Dear Mom and Dad," Bruno dictated as Boots wrote. "This sure is a great school, and my best year yet. We factored polynomials in math today. It was so fascinating that I led the applause at the end of the class.

Plans are going forward very quickly for the pool. It won't be long now.
Happily yours,
Melvin.
P.S. Everything is really great here."

"Bruno, this is the most ridiculous letter yet! Last time it was geography I was in love with. The time before that, health. My folks are going to think I've gone crazy!"

"They have to be convinced that taking you out of the Hall would ruin your life," Bruno insisted. "This is the only subtle way. Otherwise, you may as well start packing. Gobble, gobble."

Boots swallowed hard. "Have you got a stamp?"

What's on the menu?

"$844.50," Bruno announced as the last quarter clicked into the bucket. It was Sunday morning, and he and Boots were seated on the floor of their room counting the proceeds from the talent show.

"What's that dollar in your hand?" Boots asked accusingly. "Royalties for inventing the 'ugliest man in the world' skit?"

"Of course not!" Bruno replied, highly insulted. "Miss Scrimmage's is going to the Royal Ontario Museum tomorrow, and Cathy's going to buy us a lottery ticket while she's in town. A hundred thousand bucks. That'll pay for it four times over."

"I don't suppose it ever occurred to you that we might not win," Boots said.

"Not for a minute," Bruno replied serenely.

"How do we get the dollar to Cathy?"

"Same as always," Bruno told him. "We become the midnight marauders. Tonight after lights-out."

Mr. Sturgeon sat at the breakfast table staring distastefully at his jack-in-the-box. "Mildred," he said thoughtfully, "it's too bad the barracuda didn't win this thing. Everything else happened to her last night."

"Poor Miss Scrimmage," sighed Mrs. Sturgeon, pouring coffee for two. "It certainly wasn't her night. As if the eggs and the owl and the rabbit weren't enough, her well-bred young ladies proved how shy and demure they really are."

"Let's not be smug, Mildred. The reaction of our boys was nothing to be proud of. It leaves me with the problem of what to do about Bruno and Melvin."

"Why, let them continue their efforts, of course!" his wife exclaimed. "We've never had such school spirit!"

The Headmaster nodded in agreement. "Take a boy like Elmer Drimsdale," he said. "He's never taken part in anything before, and he's never had any friends. Bruno has brought him into the mainstream of things. I think all this fund-raising may be good for the school." He chuckled. "It's just not very good for Miss Scrimmage."

"Would you care for some French toast, dear?"

"No, thank you," her husband replied. "That Scrimcake you made me eat last night hasn't quite gone down yet."

* * *

A dozen or so boys were gathered around the lunch table.

"That brings our total to $1,547.65," announced Elmer Drimsdale, "which is 6.1906% of our objective. We still need $23,452.35."

"At our present rate of income," said Chris Talbot, "by the time our pool is built our arthritis will be too severe for us to be able to swim."

"Not quite," said Elmer. "At our present rate, we will have twenty-five thousand dollars in approximately eleven months, two weeks and three days. Common arthritis does not develop so rapidly."

"Don't worry," Boots put in sarcastically. "Bruno is buying a lottery ticket. We're going to win a hundred thousand."

"Oh," said Chris. "Well, that's different."

"According to the odds," said Elmer, "I calculate that we have a better chance of being stung to death by bees than of winning first prize in the lottery."

"Given a choice," said Bruno, "I'd rather win the money. By the way, why is it that not one of you is down on his knees to me for that glorious show last night? It was my idea, after all."

All the boys began chattering at once.

"Boy, those Scrimmettes!"

"Elmer stole the show!"

"The rabbit stole the show!"

"*I* stole the show!"

"The Scrimmettes!"

"Face it, Miss Scrimmage stole the show!"

"What about the Amazing Frederick's mother?"

"And when the door prize exploded in The Fish's face . . ."

"But the *Scrimmettes!*"

"Yes," said Boots soberly. "The Scrimmettes. Bruno, we haven't heard the end of that."

"It *was* memorable," Bruno agreed with a smile.

"*I'll* never forget it," seconded Wilbur Hackenschleimer from the depths of a chicken pot pie.

Bruno ignored him. "Chris," he said, "we need posters."

"You know, I *do* go to school here," Chris protested.

"You and a lot of others could end up going to school elsewhere if this campaign doesn't work," Bruno reminded him. "How about this: *Win a Contest for Macdonald Hall?*"

"Fine," Chris agreed. "Now, what are you talking about?"

"Contests," Bruno repeated. "Every cereal box, every candy bar, every magazine has them. There's money and prizes out there, and Macdonald Hall is ready to claim its share. Every single kid at this school will be entering contests. Whatever we win will go into the pool fund."

"What about Scrimmage's?" asked Mark.

"Them too," Bruno agreed. "Eight posters — six for us and two for them." He slapped one of the two buckets which formed the table's centrepiece. "Grab one, Boots. We've got to take the money to The Fish for banking."

"To his house?" Boots asked nervously.

"Well, he's not at the office. Besides, it's better at his house. Mrs. Sturgeon will be there and she'd never let him kill us."

"If it hadn't been for her and her camera," mourned Butterfingers Rampulsky, "I wouldn't have chucked four eggs at Miss Scrimmage."

This incited more laughter.

Bruno and Boots hoisted their buckets and started out of the cafeteria building. Not two steps from the door, Boots let out an unearthly howl and collapsed in his tracks, pointing wordlessly towards the sky.

"What? What? What?" asked Bruno, trying to follow the wildly pointing finger. Then he saw it. At the very top of the flagpole, its brown feathers stirring in the light breeze, was Miss Scrimmage's hat.

When their laughter had died down, Bruno finally managed to say, "We can't just leave it up there. It'll upset The Fish. Boots, you go up and get it down."

"Me? Why me? It was your precious Elmer Drimsdale who conjured up the owl that put it there! Let him go up and get it!"

"Don't argue with me," Bruno said. "We've got a chance to make some points with Miss Scrimmage. Now get up there and rescue that hat!"

Thoroughly defeated, Boots walked up to the flagpole and began to climb. A small crowd of Macdonald Hall boys started gathering on the lawn, while across the road, on a grassy hill, a group of girls was forming a cheering section.

When Boots was about three-quarters of the way to the top and the tip of the flag was tickling his face, a sudden gust of wind lifted the hat from the pole and carried it soaring through the air. It settled down gently onto the highway where it was immediately run over by a wedding procession consisting of approximately thirty beribboned cars, horns honking. The crowd cheered madly, and the last sight Boots saw before he slid, fireman fashion, to the ground was Miss Scrimmage standing on the balcony waving her arms at him.

Students from both schools converged on the road and stood looking down in great glee at the wreckage of Miss Scrimmage's hat. It was as flat as a pancake, newly decorated with white ribbon and a cardboard sign which read: *Good Luck Mary and Frank.* A group of girls picked up the hat and carried it home to their Headmistress.

"Boy!" Bruno exclaimed to Boots, "I wouldn't be in

your shoes! Is Miss Scrimmage ever mad at you! It's a good thing she doesn't have her shotgun!"

Boots began to shout, "Mad at me? Why me? I didn't do anything! You sent me up there! It's all your fault!"

"Oh, quit your crabbing," said Bruno, "and grab a bucket. We've got to go and hand in this money."

The two boys crossed the lawn to the small white cottage on the edge of the campus. "A chance to make points with Miss Scrimmage," Boots was muttering. "We made points, all right! Demerit points!"

Bruno rang the doorbell.

Mrs. Sturgeon opened the door. "Well, hello there. Come right in. We were just talking about your wonderful show." She led them into the living room. "Mr. Sturgeon is on the telephone at the moment. He'll be with you shortly."

"We've brought the money," said Bruno. "Mr. Sturgeon said he would take it up to the bank tomorrow to add it to our account." He held out the gold bankbook and a prepared deposit slip.

From the other room they overheard the Headmaster's voice. "Yes, well, thank you, Miss Scrimmage. I'll look into it right away." There was a click as he hung up the receiver, and then he appeared in the living room. "I thought I heard the doorbell," he said. "Ah, O'Neal. I just had a conversation with Miss Scrimmage and your name came up."

"The hat, sir?" Boots offered meekly.

"Yes. I'm told you threw it on the highway where it was destroyed by the traffic."

"I can explain everything, sir," said Bruno quickly.

"I'm sure you can," said the Headmaster smoothly, "but I would much rather hear O'Neal's version."

"Pole," said Boots. "Hat . . . flag . . . wind . . . road . . . wedding . . . Mary and Frank . . ."

Mr. Sturgeon held up his hand for silence. "On second thought," he said, "perhaps I'd better hear Walton's translation of all this."

"It's really very simple, sir," explained Bruno. "When Melvin saw the hat up on top of the flagpole, he wanted to do something nice for Miss Scrimmage because she got banged around so much last night. Sir, I couldn't hold him back. He was almost at the top of the pole when the wind blew the hat down onto the road. Then Mary and Frank's wedding procession came along and squashed poor Miss Scrimmage's hat. You see, sir, it was all a misunderstanding."

Mr. Sturgeon turned to look out the window in order to hide from the boys the expression that Miss Scrimmage's mishaps always brought to his face — part amusement, part disgust. When he turned back, his face was fully composed. "I see," he said. "Very well. Now, to what do I owe the honour of this visit?"

"The talent show raised $844.50," said Bruno proudly, indicating the two buckets. "We've brought the money so that you can bank it for us tomorrow." He paused. "We're still a little short, of course, but don't worry. We'll think of some other way to raise the rest."

"I'm sure you will," replied the Headmaster gravely. "Uh — a question before you go, boys. Had you seen the Scrimmettes' — uh — costumes before they went on stage?"

Both boys studied the carpet and shuffled uncomfortably.

Finally the Headmaster said, "I think I understand what happened there. You may leave. Good afternoon."

When Bruno and Boots had departed, Mr. Sturgeon turned a bewildered face to his wife and asked, "Mildred, who on earth are Mary and Frank?"

* * *

Two shadowy figures dropped to the ground from the window of room 306 and hid in the bushes until they were sure that all was clear. Bruno and Boots, each carrying a large cardboard poster, dashed across the campus and the highway, scaled the wrought-iron fence and came to a halt under the familiar window. Bruno scooped up and threw a handful of pebbles and immediately Diane's blonde head appeared.

"Come on up," she called softly.

The two boys shinnied up the drainpipe and Diane helped them over the sill and into the room.

"We were expecting you," she told them. "Cathy's off raiding the kitchen. We like to entertain in style."

The door opened and Cathy Burton appeared, wheeling a laden tea-cart in front of her. "Hi, there," she greeted them. "Good pickings tonight. Leftover roast beef, chocolate cake — help yourselves."

All four devoted the next ten minutes to the kind of serious eating perfected by Wilbur Hackenschleimer. Bruno, who had been the first to start, was the last to quit.

Finally he said, "My compliments to room service. That was great. Now to business. These are the posters for our latest fund-raising plan. The idea is to enter every single contest you can find. All winnings go into the pool fund." He reached into his pocket and pulled out a crumpled dollar bill. "This is for our lottery ticket. Buy a winner."

"I didn't know they sold lottery tickets at the Museum," Diane commented.

"They don't," said Cathy. "Everyone else is going to the Museum. We're going shopping."

Diane nodded in resignation. "I was afraid of that."

"Tell me," Boots asked, changing the subject, "did you girls get into trouble over those costumes?"

"No," Cathy said airily. "We told Miss Scrimmage that you and Bruno talked us into it."

Boots held his head and said nothing. Bruno laughed in appreciation.

"Well, we'd better get going. We'll be back tomorrow night to pick up the ticket. What's on the menu?"

"Liver," said Diane with loathing.

"We have chicken on Mondays," offered Bruno.

"Good," said Cathy. "Tomorrow night we'll visit you."

"But — " Boots protested in horror.

"See you tomorrow," said Cathy as she hustled them out the window and down the drainpipe.

* * *

"Sir, we have three new ideas for raising money, and we thought we'd better check them out with you."

Mr. Sturgeon sat back in his chair and sighed. "Go on, Walton."

"Well, sir," began Bruno, "Gormley is having a fall fair next weekend. We'd like to go and enter Wilbur Hackenschleimer in the pie-eating contest. There's a ten dollar prize and Wilbur would be a cinch."

"He can eat more pies than they can bake," Boots added.

Mr. Sturgeon had visions of himself sitting beside Wilbur in Emergency. Wilbur was having his stomach pumped. His parents had to be informed.

"I absolutely forbid it," he said firmly. "I will not permit you to play games with another boy's health."

"Well then, sir," Bruno went on, undaunted, "tomorrow night in the fifth race at Woodbine there's a horse called Cloudy Sunshine. Elmer Drimsdale figured the odds, and sir, he just can't lose! So would you take ten dollars of the pool money and bet it for us?"

"I most certainly will not!" Mr. Sturgeon exclaimed.

"But, sir! He's a long shot! We'll profit — "

"That will be quite enough, Walton. And you too, O'Neal. This money was paid to you in good faith by people who believed they were helping a pool fund. You cannot misappropriate it for purposes of gambling. I do not approve of gambling."

"Oh, well then," stammered Bruno, "we'll just have to think of something else."

Mr. Sturgeon stood up. "You said three ideas," he pointed out. "Yet you have mentioned only two. What is the third?"

"Oh, you'd hate it, sir," said Boots earnestly.

"Nevertheless, I think I'd like to hear it."

"Well, sir," Bruno began, "I thought we could have a Monte Carlo night. Nothing big, you understand — just a little blackjack, roulette, maybe a crap table or two — "

"Out!" thundered Mr. Sturgeon. "Good day."

* * *

Boots put the finishing touches on the chicken sandwiches while Bruno stirred the lemonade.

"Have you finished the letter to your folks yet?" Bruno asked.

"Oh yes," Boots assured him. "This time it was all about a French class that was *très fantastique*. To me, they're all about as subtle as a train wreck. I said my father was an athlete, not a musclehead."

"Keep it up," ordered Bruno, "or your next letter home is going to be postmarked York Academy."

"Yes, I know," said Boots. "Gobble, gobble."

"The girls should be here soon." Bruno yawned. "It's after midnight."

As if in reply, several small pebbles sailed in through the open window and landed in the lemonade. A voice from outside exclaimed, "Oops," and there was high-pitched giggling.

Bruno and Boots rushed to the window and hauled Cathy and Diane over the sill.

"Shhh!" Boots whispered frantically. "We have a House Master!"

Cathy nodded. "What's for eats? I'm starved!"

"Chicken sandwiches," said Boots.

"And lemonade on the rocks," added Bruno. "Your signal landed in the drink."

There was more giggling, followed by a sharp rapping at the door. "Walton — O'Neal — you sound like a couple of girls in there! Pipe down and go to sleep!"

When they were finished eating, Cathy handed over the lottery ticket. "Your number is 41965," she told them. "And I hope you win. We met some turkeys from York Academy in town today. They are just impossible about beating you in the swim meet!"

"Aren't you glad you kicked one of them?" Diane said with a grin.

"I guess we may as well tell you," Bruno said, "that there's a good chance Boots might end up in York Academy because of their athletic program."

Cathy slapped both hands over her mouth to suppress the screech of protest that rose from her throat. "But — but you'd be a turkey!" she managed to whisper in Boots' face.

"Yeah, well, we're working on it," Boots replied.

"Cathy, we can't stay much longer," Diane said nervously.

Cathy nodded. "We'd better split," she agreed. She turned to Bruno and Boots. "When you win the lottery, can we come swimming in your pool?"

"Only if you make your bathing suits in sewing class," Bruno grinned.

Bruno and Boots helped the girls back out over the sill and watched until they disappeared into the darkness.

Jingle fever

"This contest thing," grumbled Boots, "is costing us twenty-five G's in postage alone."

"Toss me another one of those entry forms for the *Sudso Detergent Cash Giveaway*," said Bruno. "We're bound to win if we enter enough of them."

"Cool Cola! Snuggums Longjohns! Sudso Detergent! Bibble Bubble Gum!" snorted Boots. "This is insanity!"

"It's this kind of insanity that's going to keep people like you out of places like York Academy," Bruno retorted. "We've *got* to win something. Two whole campuses are heart and soul into this campaign."

That was true. Every magazine and comic book was ripped to shreds as students searched for entry forms. Cold cereal was enjoying an unprecedented popularity at breakfast so that more boxtops would be available. Macdonald Hall's outgoing mail filled ten sacks instead of the usual two. Students were occupied with praising products in fifty words or less, and inventing catchy jingles to sell everything from toilet paper to limousines.

"I've got it!" Bruno exclaimed. "Listen to this:

> *Cool Cola tastes just great,*
> *Buy a bottle, maybe eight.*
> *If you really like the stuff,*
> *You can never get enough.*

How about that, eh?"

"Maybe eight?" Boots repeated. "What about all those numbers in between? You know, like sevens, twos, fours."

"None of them rhyme with 'great,'" said Bruno. "I'm sending it in. It's a cinch."

There was a polite knock at the door. "Am I interrupting anything?" came the timid voice of Elmer Drimsdale.

"Oh, nothing much," called Boots sarcastically. "Only the greatest jingle ever to sell a bottle of pop — or maybe eight. Come on in."

Elmer entered the room. "Could you please spare an entry blank for the Cool Cola jingle contest?" he requested. "I think I've come up with the winner."

"A tie!" crowed Boots. "We have a tie! Let's hear it."

Elmer cleared his throat:

> *"Caffeine for your addled pate,*
> *Carbohydrates for your weight,*
> *Make your thorax palpitate —*
> *Get Cool Cola by the crate."*

Without a word Bruno handed over an entry blank

and Elmer rushed off to complete it.

The scene was similar that evening in many Macdonald Hall rooms. In 107, Chris Talbot was labouring over a piece of paper.

"Hmmm. Let's see," he said slowly. *"I eat Snappy Wappies for breakfast because . . ."*

"They taste like sawdust," finished his roommate.

"Well, yes, they do," Chris admitted, "but I can't put that. So I'll put that they're delicious and they set me up for the whole day. That should win me something."

* * *

Pete Anderson leaned back in his chair and surveyed his work with great satisfaction. "I've just completed a hundred and nineteen entries for the Happy Elephant Jellybean contest," he announced to his roommate. It's that count the jellybeans in the jar thing. Surely one of my guesses has to be right."

"Mmmm," said his roommate absently. "What rhymes with refrigerator?"

* * *

"Listen to this!" said Mark Davies to Louis Brown.
> *"What a shine from Gleam-o Wax!*
> *It really takes those hits and whacks.*
> *You couldn't scratch it with an axe!*
> *A dollar ten, including tax."*

"Pretty good," admitted Louis, "but naturally it's not a match for this:
Use a Smith foot-odour pad,
And your feet won't smell so bad."

"That's touching," said Mark. "Very touching."

* * *

On construction, wrote Sidney Rampulsky, *you should always wear a hard hat because if someone drops a brick on your head and you're not wearing a hard hat you could die.*

* * *

"I think I've come up with something honest and refreshing," said Wilbur Hackenschleimer to his roommate. "It's for the Whippo Cheese Spread contest. Listen: *I love Whippo Cheese Spread because it's food and anything that's food is okay by me.* Hey, why are you laughing? What's so funny?"

* * *

I like Azgard Soap because it gets you so clean that you don't have to take another stupid bath for a month, wrote Marvin Trimble.

"A month? Boy, I'm putting in for another roommate!"

* * *

Perry Elbert was poetic. He wrote:
>'Twas a dark and stormy night
>And my heart was filled with fright.
>But everything turned out all right,
>I had my Sammy Horse night light.

* * *

The contest fever carried across the road. Miss Scrimmage's girls were hard at work filling in entry blanks and making up commercials.

"I've been using Fragrant Daisy Shampoo for forty years," read Cathy Burton, *"and never once have I had a speck of dandruff."*

"That's ridiculous," exclaimed Diane Grant. "You haven't even been alive for forty years!"

"True," said Cathy. "And it's also true that I've never been a stock-car racer, but that didn't stop me from saying how I use only XEQ Motor Oil. No matter what I have to say, Boots is staying right where he is!"

"Fine," observed Diane. "And what if you win the contest and they come here looking for a racing driver? They'll find out you're not even old enough to have a licence."

"That's why I signed Miss Scrimmage's name," Cathy replied.

The thought of Miss Scrimmage piloting a racing car was too much. They collapsed into gales of laughter.

* * *

After a few days things settled down at Macdonald Hall, and most of the boys concerned themselves solely with academic matters. With the number of available contests dwindling, Bruno racked his brain for another money-raising project and Boots continued to write glowing letters home.

On Thursday morning, before breakfast, Boots opened the door of room 306 to admit the office messenger. There was a note for Bruno and an identical one for himself. They read: *You are invited to the Headmaster's residence this afternoon at four o'clock to see photographs from the talent show. Cookies and milk will be served.* The signature was: *Mrs. Sturgeon.*

"She has to be the nicest person in the world," Boots remarked, but there was no reply. Bruno never got up for breakfast.

When he got to the dining hall, Boots found that all the boys who had appeared in the talent show had received similar invitations, and all were as pleased as he was.

At four that afternoon the cast of the talent show appeared on Mrs. Sturgeon's doorstep. Butterfingers Rampulsky tried to make himself small behind Wilbur.

He was not quite sure that he hadn't been called to account for throwing the eggs at Miss Scrimmage. But Mrs. Sturgeon was all smiles as she bustled them into her living room.

"Cookies and milk first," she said brightly. "You're all growing boys."

The boys ate happily, although they were quiet and a little shy at being invited to the Headmaster's home socially.

Mrs. Sturgeon produced a photo album from the drawer of a cabinet. "Gather around, boys, so everyone can see." The pictures broke the ice and the boys were soon chattering and laughing easily.

"Hey, there's Bruno! Look at that stupid grin!"

"Get a load of Hughie and Louie!"

"Look, Butterfingers, there you are just before you —"

"Don't say it! I know what I did!"

"Look at Hackenschleimer's muscles!"

"Wow! The Scrimmettes!"

The picture of the Amazing Frederick with his head in the fishtank got a big cheer, as did the sight of Boots being sawed in half by Marvin the Magnificent. There was even a picture of Elmer Drimsdale, his face all scrunched up, with an owl swooping down on him. This brought more hilarity to the group. But the biggest cheer of all came from the picture of the Headmaster of Macdonald Hall being attacked by his door prize.

Boots laughed until the tears ran down his cheeks. "That would win first prize in any photo contest," he declared.

Bruno looked thoughtful.

Hold that pose

"Sir, we'd like to have a funny photo contest."

Mr. Sturgeon smiled thinly. "If you two boys exhibited this kind of creative thinking in class, you would undoubtedly be the finest students in the country."

"Thank you, sir," said Bruno.

"Actually, it wasn't meant as a compliment," the Headmaster replied. "However, before I give permission for this venture, I shall have to know all the details. For the talent show I was foolish enough to give you a free hand, and quite a few surprises cropped up."

"For us too, sir," put in Boots.

"I realize that you were not totally to blame. However — tell me about your funny photo contest."

"Everyone from both schools can enter," Bruno began, "at twenty-five cents per picture, black and white only. We'll display the entries on the wall in the dining hall."

"Mark Davies has agreed to do the photo developing

at cost price," Boots continued. "And we'd like to ask Mr. Snow to judge the pictures and pick a winner and two runners-up."

"We decided on cash prizes," added Bruno. "Ten dollars for the winner, and five each for the other two."

Mr. Sturgeon thought it over. It was fairly creative, it appeared harmless, and it seemed safe enough even for Miss Scrimmage. He knew that most of his boys had cameras, and twenty-five cents was very reasonable.

"I shall agree on two conditions," he said finally. "One, that the photography lab must loan cameras to those boys who do not have them and who wish to enter. And two, that all photographs accepted and displayed must be tasteful and suitable for a school."

"Certainly, sir," Bruno assured him.

"Then we have permission?" Boots asked.

"You have permission," Mr. Sturgeon nodded. But when they left him he sat at his desk for a long time wondering if, perhaps, he were not getting a little soft.

* * *

When the door of room 107 burst open and Bruno and Boots barged in, Chris Talbot immediately reached for pad and pencil.

"What is it this time?" he asked wearily.

"A funny photo contest," Bruno replied. He and Boots filled in all the details while Chris made notes.

"I want posters everywhere," Bruno concluded. "Two for Scrimmage's and six for us ought to do it. The date will be two weeks from Saturday."

Bruno and Boots were about to leave when a terrific clattering noise from next door shook the room. It brought a big smile to the face of Boots O'Neal.

"That George and his typewriter!" Chris exclaimed in annoyance. "This goes on every day at the same time! It's like living next to a time bomb!"

"That's not a typewriter. It's a teletype machine," Boots explained. "He has to know whether Magneco is up or down."

"You're kidding!"

"I never kid about George," said Boots. "George is not funny."

"That guy is weird!" Chris exclaimed. "Well, if you'll excuse me, I have some posters to make."

* * *

The funny photo contest was received with an enthusiasm that even Bruno hadn't predicted — the faculty trip to town brought back two cases of film ordered by the students. Mark Davies recruited several helpers in anticipation of a heavy workload.

To everyone's surprise, especially the Headmaster's, the first entry was made by Mrs. Sturgeon. She entered the picture of her husband winning the door prize at the talent show. As Boots put it, "Everyone can forget first prize. That's the funniest picture I ever saw in my life!"

But then a senior named Mario Brundia entered a picture of Wilbur Hackenschleimer, his mouth open wide enough to drive a truck through, about to attack a triple-decker hamburger with the works, and Boots was not so sure.

Pictures began to pour in by the hundreds. Notable among these was a particularly good study of Coach Flynn lying on the floor in pain after demonstrating to the boys the proper way to use the vaulting horse. Someone had taken a camera to gym class. There was also a picture of Sidney Rampulsky in free fall over the newly-waxed floor of the infirmary, where he had gone for an aspirin and stayed for an ankle cast. Bruno Walton had even managed to capture on film the expression on the face of Mr. Hubert, the chemistry teacher, when someone accidentally dipped his beard in a beaker of acid. This picture was of such good quality that smoke could actually be seen rising from the tip of the beard.

And still the pictures poured in. There were so many in just five days that Bruno and Boots had to start on a second wall in the dining hall. And mealtimes at Macdonald Hall were scenes of raucous delight as the boys all rushed to see the day's entries.

To Bruno's chagrin, Boots entered a picture of his roommate in a state of peaceful slumber, the blankets in turmoil and the pillow partially over his face. To get even, Bruno snapped a still-life photo of Boots's open gym locker, crammed full of old sweat socks and wadded-up jerseys. Prominent at the top was the stenciled name, *Melvin O'Neal*.

Even Miss Scrimmage became enthusiastically involved. Unfortunately, however, she was under the impression that she was entering a serious photo contest, and when she set up her antique camera on its tripod one evening, it was to capture on film the beauty of a bowl of fruit. This was the first time in thirty years that Miss Scrimmage had used her camera, so she might be excused for grossly overloading the hand-held flash tray. She was humming happily to herself as she crept under the black hood and peered through the lens to focus.

Foom! The flash powder ignited the hood, the curtains and the upholstery. Dense clouds of white smoke poured out of the sitting room and into the hall.

"Fire!" screamed Miss Scrimmage.

Into the room burst Cathy Burton, wildly spraying foam from a fire extinguisher. She sprayed until a thick blanket of foam lay over everything, including the Headmistress. Then, satisfied that the fire was out, she whipped out her own small camera and snapped a picture of Miss Scrimmage amid the wreckage.

Diane Grant and two other girls came rushing in. "What happened?"

"Oh, nothing," Cathy said airily. "Miss Scrimmage has everything under control."

* * *

It was becoming apparent that a naturally funny picture was hard to come by and that artificial circumstances had to be created. These creations began to get a little out of hand.

"Elmer," said Bruno, "I want to buy that poster of the Pacific salmon from you."

"Oh, you can have it for free," replied Elmer. "I have fifteen more in my dresser. I'm really glad to see you're taking an interest in icthyology."

"Right," Bruno nodded. He picked up the poster and smashed it over Elmer's head, leaving it hanging around his neck. Then he pulled out his instamatic and snapped a picture.

* * *

Pete Anderson was walking across the campus to his first class one morning when he was suddenly struck in the centre of the forehead by a suction-cup arrow which vibrated for a moment and stuck there. From behind a clump of bushes jumped Boots O'Neal, the bow over his shoulder, his camera in his hand. *Snap.*

And when a furious Pete began to chase Boots, Wilbur Hackenschleimer was on hand to capture the chase on film.

100

* * *

Perry Elbert was splashing happily in a bubble bath one evening when his roommate appeared, thrust a rubber duck into his arms and snapped a picture.

Things were getting worse. When Wilbur Hackenschleimer put his football helmet on at practice one afternoon, cold spaghetti spilled down over his head. Bruno Walton just happened to be there with his camera.

* * *

Mark Davies woke up one morning to find his face painted with peanut butter and jelly, and a slice of bread attached to his hair with a sprig of parsley and a toothpick. Another slice of bread was taped under his chin. His roommate photographed him in this state, and although he was angry, Mark was honour-bound to develop the picture for entry into the contest.

* * *

Miss Scrimmage's also had its share of troubles over the photo contest.

When Miss Smedley, the gym teacher, was showing

her class how to jog without becoming exhausted, she failed to notice that Cathy Burton had attached a small smoke bomb to the back of her shorts. Miss Smedley ran around the cinder track leaving a plume of smoke behind her like the vapour trail of a supersonic jet. Cathy took the picture.

When Cathy was put on kitchen duty as punishment for this escapade, she didn't see Diane Grant sneak in and add half a box of detergent to the dishwasher. Diane took a picture of Cathy, knee-deep in suds, vainly trying to stem the overflow with her bare hands.

For revenge, Cathy knotted all Diane's underwear together and photographed her, perplexed and astonished, pulling miles of it out of her drawer.

There were also pictures of girls caught unawares arm-wrestling, smoking cigars and drooling toothpaste. No one was immune.

* * *

By now three walls of the cafeteria were covered with pictures — and more were coming in. The inexpensive little contest was turning into a huge moneymaker, as most students were entering several photographs. And the schemes for creating humorous subjects were getting wilder.

Rob Adams reported to the infirmary, apparently permanently stuck to his desk chair.

Marvin Trimble's paper cup of tomato juice exploded in the dining room and the culprit proved to be, of all people, Elmer Drimsdale, who was brilliant even in making miniature bombs.

Bruno Walton found out, the hard way, that his soup was full of hot chili peppers. The photographer turned out to be Perry Elbert, who had never been happier than when he took that particular photograph.

Someone planted a tape recorder inside the skeleton in the science room. When the instructor opened the case, the grinning skeleton wished him good morning and a flashbulb went off to record his astonishment.

When Chris Talbot returned to his room after dinner one night, he was pushed by mysterious hands into a child's wading pool which had materialized in his doorway. His freshman roommate snapped the picture. The resulting shouting match caused their next-door neighbour, George Wexford-Smyth III, to spill his after-dinner medicine, the one he took every evening to neutralize the germs he may have picked up during the course of the day.

"This is the last straw!" George cried. "The whole campus is insane! I'm going to the Headmaster!"

* * *

The next day during lunch, Mr. Sturgeon appeared in the dining hall and called for order.

"The photo contest is officially over as of this moment," he announced. "There will be no more practical jokes, and the next boy who so much as clicks the shutter of a camera will wash dishes for a full month. Photographs which have already been taken, including those from Miss Scrimmage's school, may be processed and entered but there are to be no more. Judging will take place on Saturday as scheduled, and when Mr. Snow arrives to do the judging, this campus had better be on its best behaviour. That is all. Good afternoon."

So things returned to normal at Macdonald Hall.

* * *

Mr. Snow arrived early, and it was fortunate that he did, because there were over four thousand pictures for him to examine. He took his duties seriously and spent hours in the Board Room of the Faculty Building. Occasionally Mr. Sturgeon and Mrs. Davis could hear rumblings of laughter coming from behind the closed door. Apparently the Chairman of the Board found some of the photographs extremely funny.

The day was warm and sunny, and an informal assembly was arranged for both schools on the north lawn of Macdonald Hall. Portable microphone in hand, Mr. Snow stood up before the assembled students.

"First of all, I would like to congratulate all of you

who participated in this wonderful contest. I wish I had prizes for everyone. Before I announce the three winners, I would like to make honourable mention of the following: Melvin O'Neal for his picture of a boy with an arrow stuck to his forehead; Mortimer Day for his picture of a boy taking a bubble bath with a rubber duck; Bruno Walton for his picture of Mr. Hubert with his beard on fire; and Louis Brown for his picture of a boy made up to look like some kind of sandwich. I would also like to mention that Miss Scrimmage's photograph of a fruit bowl was very nice indeed."

There was thunderous applause for the honourable mentions.

"And now," said Mr. Snow, "I would like — "

The proceedings were interrupted by the sudden arrival of a huge transport truck. Its motor roared as it backed up the driveway, the horn honking vigorously. Mr. Sturgeon, followed by most of the student body, went over to the truck. The driver jumped down from the cab. "This here Macdonald Hall?"

"Yes, it is," said the Headmaster. "May I help you?"

"Got a couple of crates here for a Peter Anderson," said the driver.

Pete pushed his way to the front. "For me?"

"Yup. Sign here." The driver handed Pete the delivery slip.

Pete stared. "One hundred pounds of jellybeans?"

"That's right," confirmed the driver. He indicated

two enormous crates on the back of his load. "Where do you want these?"

Pete looked helplessly at Mr. Sturgeon.

"Ah — yes," said the Headmaster finally. "Just leave them here, please. We'll decide what to do with them later."

The driver unloaded the crates and got back into his cab. As the big transport made its way out to the highway, Mr. Sturgeon turned to Pete.

"Anderson," he said, "would it be presumptuous of me to ask where you acquired one hundred pounds of jellybeans?"

"The Happy Elephant contest, sir," said Pete. "I guess I must have won first prize."

"Well," said the Headmaster, "after the assembly you'll have to find a place for your jellybeans."

"Oh, they're not mine, sir. I won them for Macdonald Hall. For the pool fund."

Bruno Walton pushed his way to Pete's side. "You see, sir, we've all been entering contests to win stuff for our fund."

"Pool construction companies rarely accept payment in jellybeans," commented the Headmaster in amusement. "It would appear that our students will be eating jellybeans for a very long time." He raised his voice slightly. "Back to your places, everyone. We must conclude our program."

The students resumed their places for the remainder of the assembly.

"And now for the winners," Mr. Snow went on when all had settled down. "When your name is called, please come up to collect your prize. The first of our runners-up is Elmer Drimsdale for his picture of what appears to be an explosion at the dinner table."

Elmer was cheered as Mr. Snow presented him with his five dollar prize.

"Our other runner-up is Mrs. Sturgeon for her excellent photograph of a Jack-in-the-box going off in Mr. Sturgeon's face.

As this was a very popular entry, the ovation was tremendous.

"And our ten dollar grand prize goes to Catherine Burton for her photograph of Miss Scrimmage, which I will not attempt to describe and do not presume to understand. I only know that it is the funniest thing I have ever seen."

Screaming all the way, Cathy collected her prize. At Pete's suggestion, one of the jellybean crates was opened and the students helped themselves. The funny photo contest was over.

* * *

"Dear Mom and Dad," Boots read aloud from his letter. *"This is the best school year of my life. Yesterday I got*

an *A+ on my English composition. It was entitled 'Why I Love Macdonald Hall.' Not only that, but in math I learned how to bisect an angle without even using a protractor.*

"I'm really glad that we're starting to have more health food in the cafeteria. I love wheat-germ muffins. Good eating is part of our training program for when the pool is ready.
Joyfully yours,
Melvin."

"Very good," Bruno approved. "You keep your folks happy and I keep raising money — and we'll both be at Macdonald Hall forever."

Is this considered our fault?

"According to Elmer Drimsdale, sir," said Bruno, "we have $2,550.90. Elmer says that's 10.2036% of what we need, leaving us still to collect $22,449.10."

Mr. Sturgeon smiled. "I would not presume to question the calculations of Elmer Drimsdale. Well, boys, I find it remarkable that you have actually managed to raise ten percent of the money in so short a time. And that does not include Anderson's jellybeans. A truck arrived this morning with another seventy-five pounds of them, representing second and third prizes in the Happy Elephant contest. One can only hope that none of the other students were quite as thorough as the Anderson boy."

"Well, sir," said Bruno reflectively, "every little bit helps. They say the first ten percent is the hardest. The other ninety should come easy as pie."

There was a low moan from Boots.

Mr. Sturgeon settled back in his chair. "May I take

that to mean you have another brilliant scheme on the drawing board?"

"Yes, sir," said Bruno eagerly. "You see, we have lots of really good workers, but the ideas are coming only from Melvin and me. I was thinking of something like an Individual Effort Day when anyone from either school could set up a booth and make money any way he or she wanted."

"It would be really great, sir," Boots added as he felt Bruno's elbow in his ribs. "There would be a lot more kids participating."

"And we'd make a fortune," Bruno concluded.

Mr. Sturgeon thought it over. He had checked with the teachers and had been assured that all students were maintaining their standards. As a matter of fact, grades were a little higher and the number of misdemeanors lower. None of the students wanted to be assigned extra tutoring or punishment for fear of missing something to do with the fund-raising campaign. All things considered, the campaign had been very good for the school.

"I shall allow an Individual Effort Day," the Headmaster said at last. "However, you two will be the judges of what is and is not suitable. You are aware of the standards of Macdonald Hall. What date do you have in mind?"

"A week from Saturday, sir," said Bruno. "That gives everybody ten days to prepare."

"All right, then. Good day."

For the next ten days, Macdonald Hall became the strangest place around. The boys hardly talked to each other for fear of accidentally giving away their plans to someone else. Posters advertising Individual Effort Day were all over the Hall and Miss Scrimmage's too. The wood shop vibrated to the sounds of hammers and saws building booths and mysterious contraptions. Out of Elmer Drimsdale's room came strange noises. A whole new lingo sprang up.

"Get out of my room and close the door behind you!"

"Who took my monkey wrench?"

"That's my history notes you just poured all that grease on!"

"What the heck is Drimsdale doing?"

"If you steal my idea, I'll hit you with this board!"

"Turn up the radio so Kevin won't be able to hear what we're saying!"

"It took me five days to build what you just sat on!"

"Oh no! It collapsed!"

"Elmer, come out of there!"

A great deal of spying took place, and a great deal of counter-espionage as well. Outside Sidney Rampulsky's room, Pete Anderson was caught lurking in the bushes with a periscope. He got a crutch over the head for his efforts. When Mark Davies opened his closet door one night, there stood Perry Elbert with notepad, pencil and guilty face. Wilbur Hackenschleimer received a nasty black eye while peering through the keyhole into Rob Adams' room. Rob threw open the door too suddenly for Wilbur to get out of the way.

The only boy untroubled by the spying was Elmer Drimsdale. Before starting on his project Elmer had effectively booby-trapped all entrances to his room, and everyone knew about it. Bruno, mostly out of curiosity, had tried to get inside and could attest to the fact that room 201 was a fortress. At the window he was sprayed with water and hopelessly tangled in a net. At the door he received a jarring electric shock.

With the responsibility for law and order resting on their shoulders, Bruno and Boots were greatly relieved when the big day finally arrived.

* * *

Mr. and Mrs. Sturgeon stepped out onto their front porch into the warm autumn sunshine.

"William, did you bring money?"

"Yes, Mildred," her husband replied. "I'm beginning to feel that I am personally supplying the pool fund."

"Must you always be so cranky about everything?" she sighed. "The boys and girls have worked so hard for all this. Let's enjoy it."

The first booth they came to was operated by Mark

Davies, who was doing a big business. A sign proclaimed: *Your Name in the Headlines — 50¢.* Using the Macdonald Hall newspaper, Mark was printing custom headlines. As the Headmaster watched, Chris walked away well pleased with his headline, which said, *Christopher Talbot Spends 10 Days Locked in Meat Freezer.* Mrs. Sturgeon finally emerged from the line carrying a newspaper which read: *William R. Sturgeon Wins Heavyweight Championship.* She was giggling. He knew right then and there that she was planning to spend money at every single booth so that no one would feel left out.

They stopped to buy some cookies from Diane Grant, who was in charge of a baked-goods booth.

"Scrim-cookies, no doubt," Mr. Sturgeon commented.

"Why, how did you know, sir?" exclaimed Diane.

"Lucky guess," smiled the Headmaster.

Next they came upon a display called *Sponge Throw.* Boots O'Neal was sitting on a chair with a bucket full of wet sponges in front of him. Six yards away stood Bruno Walton, behind a sheet of plywood. Bruno's head peeped through a hole in the wood.

"Would you like to try, sir?" Boots asked. "For a nickel you can throw a sponge at Bruno."

Mr. Sturgeon instantly produced a quarter. "I'll start with five," he said, positively grinning. With a swift overhand motion, he threw five direct hits that left

Bruno sputtering. "I played a little cricket at university," he explained with great satisfaction.

"Wow!" said Boots admiringly. "I'm glad it was Bruno's turn instead of mine."

"Oh?" said Mr. Sturgeon. "You are to have a turn too? In that case, I shall be back."

As the Headmaster stepped out of the way, Perry Elbert was next in line. Perry handed Boots a dollar bill. He did not ask for change.

The Headmaster and his wife went along stopping at every display. Mr. Sturgeon had his caricature done at Chris Talbot's booth, and was a little shocked to see how cold and stern his eyes were. Mrs. Sturgeon bought a bouquet of paper flowers from some of Miss Scrimmage's girls. They each paid the dime entry fee and went in to view Marvin Trimble's rock collection.

They had just bought lemonade from two boys when they heard a familiar scream.

Mr. Sturgeon nudged his wife. "It's Miss Scrimmage. She's in there." He pointed to a tent with a sign on it that announced, *Cathy's Chamber of Horrors.* As they approached, Cathy Burton came out of the tent leading a hysterical Miss Scrimmage.

"They weren't real snakes, Miss Scrimmage," the girl was saying. "And the great white shark was just an illusion. It's all right. Really it is. You're safe now."

Eventually Miss Scrimmage calmed down and joined the Sturgeons on their tour of the grounds.

By far the most popular booth was Elmer Drimsdale's. The most carefully guarded secret of the whole affair turned out to be an enormous coin-operated pinball machine.

"Oh, look, William! Isn't that marvellous!" exclaimed Mrs. Sturgeon. "You must play it!"

"I consider it gambling, Mildred," her husband replied primly. "I do not approve of any form of gambling."

Mrs. Sturgeon slapped a dime into his hand and pushed him up to Elmer's wonderful machine. "Don't be a fuddy-duddy!" she whispered. "Play!"

Mr. Sturgeon inserted the dime and the machine sprang to life. Bells rang, lights flashed, and the ball sped around the board.

Twenty minutes and many dimes later, Mrs. Sturgeon approached her husband. "William," she said in a low tone. "You're hogging the machine. There's a long line-up behind you."

Mr. Sturgeon did not even turn around. "There is an art to pinball, Mildred," he said abstractedly as he operated the flippers. "It requires complete concentration. If you hadn't disturbed me, I would have won a free game."

"Oh, come away from there!" she exclaimed, dragging him off by the arm. "There's so much more to see."

Miss Scrimmage paid twenty-five cents for a grab-bag package which turned out to be a complete set of bubble gum cards covering the 1976 World Series. She kindly assured the worried vendor that she was perfectly satisfied with her prize. "After all," she said, "I have been a Rocket Richard fan for years."

Wilbur Hackenschleimer was doing very well as inventor and operator of the afternoon's only ride. This consisted of a padded barrel at the top of a small hill. The rider would climb into the barrel and Wilbur would roll it down the hill into a pit of sand. The only mishap of the day occurred when the rider, Coach Flynn, sneezed in transit and put the barrel off course. It missed the sand pit, rolled across the lawn, bounced over the ditch, hurtled across the highway where it narrowly missed collision with a sightseeing bus, and came to rest in Miss Scrimmage's chrysanthemum bed. An enthusiastic Mr. Flynn emerged from the barrel to find, to his amazement, that Individual Effort Day was gone. Had it ended during his ride? He was set straight when Wilbur rushed up, concerned for the safety of his barrel.

Mr. Sturgeon became annoyed watching his wife and Miss Scrimmage throw nickels into a saucer attempting to win a prize. He nudged them aside. "Here is how it is done," he said quietly. He threw and missed. Missed again. And again. "I am going to do it," he said between clenched teeth, "if I have to spend a hundred dollars!" It only cost him two. His prize was a huge gift-wrapped carton which he was obliged to lug around for the remainder of the afternoon.

They paid a quarter each to see a puppet show run by two Macdonald Hall boys. The show was about a wicked Headmaster who had a swimming pool and a nice Headmaster who didn't. In the end, the King took the pool away from the wicked Headmaster and gave it to the nice one. The nice Headmaster and his nice boys lived happily ever after.

Mr. Sturgeon was extremely amused. "The wicked Headmaster is Hartley of York Academy," he explained to Miss Scrimmage.

"Oh, and who is the nice Headmaster?" she asked innocently.

Mrs. Sturgeon bought a sign hand-lettered by a talented associate of Chris Talbot:

Don't be a foole
Support ye poole.

The afternoon was drawing to a close and the Sturgeons, accompanied by Miss Scrimmage, began to wend their way towards home, when suddenly the Headmaster remembered his promise to return to the sponge throw. This time Bruno was taking money and Boots was the target. Mr. Sturgeon produced another quarter and picked up the first sponge.

"Oh, this is violent," said Miss Scrimmage. "I think I'll go over and see how the bake table is doing."

Mr. Sturgeon wound up and caught Boots flush in the face.

"Dead-ly!" Bruno cheered.

Mr. Sturgeon reached for another sponge and took careful aim. Now that he had a reputation to protect, he did not want to miss. He brought his arm forward and let fly just as Miss Scrimmage wandered absent-mindedly into the line of fire. *Splat!* The sopping sponge hit her right on the side of the head.

Bruno raced out with a towel and caught the teetering Miss Scrimmage.

"Sir," called Boots anxiously, "is this considered our fault?"

"No," said Mr. Sturgeon with just a trace of amusement in his voice. "I did that myself." Determined to get his money's worth, he threw three more direct hits at Boots.

The crowd began to thin out and the booths began to close. Before the dinner bell rang, Individual Effort Day had drawn to a successful end.

* * *

Mr. Sturgeon struggled into the house with his enormous prize. "This had better be something good," he said sourly. "It cost me over two dollars."

"Well, open it, dear," said his wife. "Let's see what you won."

In an attempt to deposit the bulky package on the coffee table in the living room, Mr. Sturgeon lost his grip on it. It hit the floor with a bang. There was movement within the box, and suddenly a voice, muffled by the wrapping, said, "Hi there! My name is Jack!"

"Mildred, how did this happen?"

"I knew you hated it, William," she explained, "so I gave it to the boys for Individual Effort Day."

"And I won it," he said softly. "I won it again."

"Yes, dear."

"Take it away, Mildred," the Headmaster ordered. "Put it where I won't have to see it — or hear it — ever again!"

* * *

"$1,437.39!" exclaimed Bruno Walton to Boots and Elmer as he dropped the last penny into bucket number six. "That's the best we've ever done!"

Elmer produced a ten dollar bill. "The Cool Cola Company sent me this," he said proudly. "It's a special consolation prize. They said my jingle was the most unusual one in the history of the company."

"Here's Sidney's two dollars," Boots put in, dropping two one dollar bills into the bucket. "It seems he coloured in the magic peanut in the ad for Ace Nuts."

Elmer looked thoughtful. "We now have $4,000.29, which is sixteen point — "

"All right, Elmer," Bruno cut in. "We know we're still short. But wasn't it a great day?"

"It sure was," said Boots. "Especially when Miss Scrimmage got hit by a wet sponge and The Fish couldn't even blame it on us."

"I wonder," mused Bruno, "if we couldn't start building the pool now. We could give the builder our $4,000.29 as a down payment and pay off the rest later."

"Much later," said Boots. "About two hundred years later."

"Before a mortgage company would consider your application," said Elmer, "you would need to show a steady source of income. Presently, you are too much of a risk."

"Oh well, grab a couple of buckets, you guys," ordered Bruno, not in the least discouraged. "Let's get this money to The Fish for banking." He grinned at Boots. "You've got a letter to write."

"Oh no!" moaned Boots. "Not another one!"

"Your parents haven't heard yet about that fabulous history class you attended recently," Bruno told him. "And if they don't hear about it, it could mean the turkey farm."

"Let's hurry," Boots agreed.

There was a loud crash at the door.

"They're here! They're here! They're here! I won!" someone cried. Bruno, Boots and Elmer rushed out of the room to see what was going on. They were nearly trampled in a stampede.

"I won!" cried the voice again. "They're here with my refrigerator!"

Bruno's eyes met Boots's. "Let's go!"

They dashed out of the dormitory, leaving a confused Elmer Drimsdale in charge of the money buckets.

Lucky Donald McHall

"We're well over the four thousand mark, sir," said Bruno.

"I have seen the figures in your bank statement," said Mr. Sturgeon. "Twenty-nine cents over, isn't it?"

"$450.29," Bruno said happily. "Mr. and Mrs. Stratton are buying Rob Adams' refrigerator. And there's plenty more where that came from."

Mr. Sturgeon leaned back. "The — uh — plenty more is what I have been wanting to discuss with you. Sit down, boys — no, not on the bench. The chairs will do." He paused to collect his thoughts. "So far you have been extremely successful with your fund-raising. However, you must face the fact that most of the money is coming from the same pockets — those of our own students and staff. In the past week I have been receiving telephone calls and letters from many of the parents complaining that their sons are repeatedly sending home for more money. It simply will not do."

"But, sir," argued Bruno, "a lot of the money from the rummage sale came from outside the school. And there's the contest prizes. And then there's Miss Scrimmage's."

"Yes," replied the Headmaster, "but the bulk of what you have came from the Macdonald Hall students. As for the contests, luck is a very fickle thing. You *have* been lucky, but you cannot seriously expect any more revenue from contests. The point that I am making is not open to argument, Walton. It is this: our own resources have been tapped and tapped again. I cannot allow it to go any further."

"Does this mean we're not allowed to raise any more money?" asked Boots anxiously. He saw himself packing for York Academy.

"Not exactly," said the Headmaster. "But in future, any funds raised will have to come from outside sources."

Bruno cleared his throat carefully. "As a matter of fact, sir, we just so happen to have a hundred dollars coming to us from an outside source." From his shirt pocket he produced a lottery ticket and a crumpled newspaper clipping. "We matched the last four digits."

Mr. Sturgeon's eyes glared with cold disapproval. "You are well aware of my feelings concerning gambling," he said. "I fail to recall giving my consent for the purchase of a lottery ticket. May I ask how you came by the ticket?"

"One of the girls from Miss Scrimmage's bought it for us when they went into town," Bruno confessed.

"And no doubt she sent it to you here by mail," Mr. Sturgeon added sarcastically. "Let me see the ticket." He examined it carefully. It was made out in the name of Donald McHall at the school's address, and was indeed a $100 winner. "Why Donald McHall?" he asked finally.

"Well, Cathy — uh — the girl just put it down that way," Bruno explained. "You know, Macdonald Hall — Donald McHall . . ."

"Yes, yes, I understand." The Headmaster sighed. "Since the money belongs to the pool fund, I shall collect it this afternoon when I am in town."

"Thank you, sir," said Boots.

"Sir," said Bruno, "I have an idea about how we can raise money from other sources. It's fruit harvest time, and we could set up a rent-a-student service for the farmers around here. We could take a couple of weeks off school and — "

"That will do," interrupted Mr. Sturgeon. "Your parents did not register you at Macdonald Hall to turn you into farm labourers."

"Yes, sir," chorused Bruno and Boots.

* * *

A dejected Bruno Walton sat on the small hill on

Macdonald Hall's front lawn and stared absently at the cars going by. There was no way, no way at all, that the school could have a pool now.

A figure approached and sat down beside him. "Bruno," said Boots, "you've been sitting here for over an hour. There's just no way. We gave it a try and it can't be done. Maybe it'll all work out."

"And maybe it won't!" Bruno growled. "And that'll leave a lot of good Macdonald Hall students sitting in York Academy or some other rotten place. It'll break up a lot of pretty good friendships too — like ours, for instance."

"That's what gets me!" Boots exclaimed. "Our school is better than York Academy even without a pool."

Bruno nodded. "It is, you know," he agreed. "That's why I just can't stand to think of those turkeys lording it over us — " He stopped dead and sat up straight. "Our school *is* better than theirs. Boots," he said with sudden new life, "look at all the cars that pass by here. Those people get to look at our beautiful school — for free!"

Boots laughed. "What are you going to do? Set up a tollbooth and charge them for the privilege?"

"As a matter of fact, that's a wonderful idea!"

"Bruno, are you *crazy?*" Boots cried. "The Fish would never give permission for that!"

"We don't have to ask him," Bruno replied earnestly. "He's already told us to go out and make money from other sources. The passing public is another source."

Boots held his head. "Bruno, this time we're going too far! If we got caught at this, we'd be lucky if York Academy would even have us!"

Bruno ignored him. "Come on!" he said excitedly. "We're going to see Wilbur!"

They dashed across the campus in the direction of Dormitory 1, raced inside and knocked on Wilbur's door. The big boy had been doing his homework.

"Wilbur, we need your help," said Bruno, getting right to the point. "We need you to borrow two sawhorses out of the wood shop without telling Mr. Lautrec."

"Why can't I tell Mr. Lautrec?"

"Because," explained Bruno, "he'll want to know what you're going to use them for and I don't want to tell him."

Wilbur, who was not very adventurous, turned pale. "But what if I get caught?"

"Don't," Bruno advised him. "Then you won't have to worry about such things. Paint the sawhorses white and meet us down by the highway at nine o'clock tonight." He turned to Boots. "Come on. We've got to go see Chris."

Down the hall they ran into Chris Talbot, who had just returned from the library.

"Two signs," said Bruno. "We need them for tonight at nine. White background, black lettering, about one yard by half a yard."

126

"Saying?" Chris prompted.

"Stop. Pay Toll. 25¢"

Chris stared at Bruno in disbelief. "Are you out of your mind? You're not going to stop cars and make them pay us a quarter?"

"Oh, yes I am!" laughed Bruno Walton.

* * *

Mr. Sturgeon had every piece of identification he owned spread out on the counter.

"The way I see it, your name is Sturgeon, not McHall," said the clerk.

"That is what I have been telling you," said Mr. Sturgeon. "I am the Headmaster of Macdonald Hall. You see, there is no such person as Donald McHall."

"Then why is the ticket made out to him?" the girl asked, eyeing Mr. Sturgeon suspiciously.

"It is simply a pseudonym for Macdonald Hall," Mr. Sturgeon explained for at least the third time. "The ticket belongs to the students of Macdonald Hall, and I am acting as their agent to collect their money for them."

"Are you sure?" the clerk asked dubiously.

"Young woman," said Mr. Sturgeon icily, "I assure you that if I should ever attempt to defraud an agency of the government of Ontario, it would not be for the paltry sum of a hundred dollars. I should, as they say, go for the bundle."

She frowned. "Are you sure Mr. McHall can't come down to claim the money himself?"

"Positive," said Mr. Sturgeon sadly.

"Well, since he seems to have given you his ticket, I guess it'll be all right," she said at last.

Mr. Sturgeon breathed a deep sigh of relief and cursed Bruno and Boots in his heart for putting him through this.

* * *

By half past nine, two gleaming white sawhorses stood blocking both the north- and southbound lanes of Highway 48, their signs proclaiming in both directions: *Stop. Pay Toll. 25¢.* Bruno and Boots were manning the northbound lane, and Wilbur and Chris the southbound. The tollbooth was ready for operation.

Boots, Chris and Wilbur were only there out of loyalty to Bruno. All three were absolutely terrified. Bruno, on the other hand, rubbed his hands with glee when he spied headlights coming along in his lane.

"Oh, boy! Our first customer."

"It had better not be a police car," called Chris from across the road. "I'm positive this is illegal!"

Boots, who had very sharp night vision, squinted at the car and went white to the ears. "It's The Fish!"

Uncharacteristically, Bruno panicked. "Run for your

life!" he cried and made a break for his own dormitory. Chris and Wilbur stood frozen, but Boots was hot on Bruno's tail. They ran only a short way.

"Hold it! Hold everything!" Bruno gasped. "We can't take off like this! We've got to go back and save Wilbur and Chris from The Fish!"

"Who's going to save *us?*" demanded Boots as they trotted back towards the scene of the crime.

"Shut up and keep running," Bruno tossed over his shoulder.

"Hide, Wilbur!" exclaimed Chris, unfrozen at last. The two boys took off towards Miss Scrimmage's apple orchard, but not before the headlights of the approaching car had clearly illuminated Wilbur Hackenschleimer's bulk clambering over the fence.

Mr. Sturgeon veered over to the soft shoulder of the road, got out of his car and surveyed the scene. He crossed the highway, eased himself gingerly over the wire fence and stepped into the shadow of the trees.

"Talbot — Hackenschleimer — come out this instant."

Chris and Wilbur shuffled out from behind a row of trees and stood shamefaced and shaking before their Headmaster.

"You both have a lot of explaining to do," Mr. Sturgeon said sternly, "but the first order of business is to remove that abomination from the highway. Let us now — "

He was interrupted by a piercing wail. Then Miss Scrimmage's voice came over the public address system. "Intruder alert! Intruder alert! All girls to remain in their rooms. Do not be afraid. You are protected."

There was a rustling sound in the underbrush behind Mr. Sturgeon. Crack! The Headmaster dropped to the ground. Over him, brandishing a softball bat, stood Cathy Burton.

"Oops!"

Bruno and Boots burst onto the scene. "Cathy, you clouted The Fish!" Boots exclaimed.

Bruno dropped to his knees beside his fallen Headmaster. "Sir! Sir, speak to me!"

Boom!

Mr. Sturgeon sat bolt upright. "Good Lord, she's got her shotgun back! Flat on the ground! Everyone!"

Miss Scrimmage appeared in the orchard, carrying a flashlight in one hand and the shotgun in the other. The bright beam illuminated Mr. Sturgeon, Cathy and the four boys all lying on the ground.

"Mercy, I've killed them!" she cried, and fainted.

Diane Grant's white face peered out from behind a nearby tree. "Cathy, is it safe to come out yet?" she whispered.

"Sir, are you sure you're all right?" asked Bruno anxiously.

"Miss Scrimmage, wake up!" Cathy was begging over and over again. "No one is dead!"

Headmaster and Headmistress faced one another. Mr. Sturgeon was livid. "What do you *mean* by firing that weapon? You could have killed one of my boys!"

"How dare you shout at me, sir?" Miss Scrimmage replied, outraged. "You were prowling in my orchard! I could have you arrested for terrorizing a defenceless woman and her innocent girls!"

"Come along, boys." Mr. Sturgeon summoned up what remained of his dignity. He herded the four boys out of the orchard, over the fence and onto the highway. There an appalling sight met his eyes. From both north and south, cars were lined up at the toll gate as far as the eye could see. Some of the drivers were beginning to get restless, and the occasional horn could be heard.

"Take those barriers down at once!" Mr. Sturgeon ordered, holding his head gingerly. The boys ran to remove the sawhorses which had backed up the traffic.

"Now," the Headmaster said when they were back on their own grounds, "go to your rooms and remain there. I wish to see Walton and O'Neal at precisely eight o'clock tomorrow morning in my office. Talbot and Hackenschleimer will be dealt with later."

"Yes, sir," said Bruno. He turned dark anxious eyes on the Headmaster. "Sir, are you absolutely sure you're all right? Maybe we'd better take you home."

"Do as you are told!" Mr. Sturgeon roared with more anger than he had ever expressed to anyone.

* * *

"We've finally done it, Bruno," said Boots miserably, holding his head in his hands as he sat on his bed. "We've gotten into trouble before, but this time nothing can keep us from being expelled. I'm doomed! My folks will kill me! Even York Academy is beginning to look good!"

"Boots," said Bruno calmly, "we've been through a heck of a lot together. If we ever needed each other for support, it's now, so let's not argue or go to pieces. We haven't been expelled yet."

"We might as well give up," said Boots. "The Fish will never let us get away with this. I told you it was crazy. How do you get such ideas?"

"It was your idea," Bruno defended himself. "Remember? You said — "

"You know I wasn't serious!" Boots lay back in surrender. "We may as well go to sleep," he said. "Whatever happens I guess just plain happens."

"That's the spirit!" said Bruno. "Never worry about what you can't avoid. Wake me at quarter to eight. Goodnight."

* * *

"Here are the groceries, Mildred," said Mr. Sturgeon,

placing a paper bag on the kitchen counter.

"Oh, thank you, dear. I needed some — William! Whatever happened to you?" Her husband was a rumpled, bedraggled sight — and there was a lump on his head.

"Oh, nothing much," Mr. Sturgeon said bitterly. "I was only stopped at an illegal toll gate set up on the road by those boys you're so proud of for their school spirit; then I was physically assaulted with a baseball bat by one of those well-bred young ladies belonging to the barracuda who, incidentally, opened fire on me — the police have returned her shotgun, can you imagine that? No one is safe!" He opened the closet to put away his coat. "Other than that, nothing happened to me!"

From the closet shelf a box slipped down and struck him on his already tender head. The lid flipped open, a soft object popped out and a recorded voice said, "Hi there! My name is Jack!"

"Mildred . . ."

The secret ingredient

The bench in the Headmaster's office was especially uncomfortable that morning. Bruno and Boots sat, hands nervously folded in their laps, waiting for Mr. Sturgeon to pronounce sentence upon them. It did not raise their hopes to see that he wore a bandage around his head and appeared to be in an irritable mood.

"I don't suppose it occurred to either of you that what you were doing is against the law."

Bruno and Boots remained silent.

"Did you take any money from passing motorists?"

"No sir," said Bruno. "Your car was the first one to come along."

"Well, thank goodness for that, anyway," said the Headmaster. "You did not actually break the law then. But you certainly intended to. Specifically, receiving money under false pretenses constitutes fraud. And that is very serious."

Boots's stomach growled noisily. He had been too

nervous to eat breakfast.

Mr. Sturgeon paused to allow his words to sink in, and then continued. "This time you have not only got yourselves into serious trouble, but you have also corrupted two boys whose previous records were spotless. I wish to know what part Hackenschleimer and Talbot played in this escapade."

"It was all my fault, sir," said Bruno steadily. "I got Chris to make the signs and Wilbur to get the saw horses, and at the last minute I talked them into working the tollbooth. I'm completely to blame, sir."

"And me," Boots added quickly.

Mr. Sturgeon nodded and began to tell Bruno and Boots what he had been telling himself ever since the swim meet. "This entire fund-raising campaign was sparked by the lowest of motives — jealousy. You have kept it going by feeding this jealousy, and I blame myself for not putting a stop to it sooner. Your aim is not so much to have a pool because you want one as to have a pool because *they* have one. That attitude is childish and unworthy of you.

"And now, your punishment. At seven each morning you will report to the kitchen to assist the staff in any duties they may find for you. During the noon hour you will do the same. At four in the afternoon you will pick up every scrap of litter on the campus until five, when you will report to the kitchen once more to assist in the serving of dinner. You will eat all your meals in the kitchen. After dinner, from seven-thirty to nine, you are assigned to wash dishes without the usual payment. Since it is autumn, you will spend your weekends raking leaves. After nine in the evenings you are confined to your room where you will do your homework and prepare the five thousand word essay which I am assigning. The subject — fraud."

The Headmaster stopped for breath. "In case this schedule leaves you any time for privileges, I hereby revoke them all. This punishment will apply until further notice. The fund-raising campaign, of course, is over. If you are caught raising money, you will be expelled. Is that clear?"

"Yes, sir."

"Then," said Mr. Sturgeon, glancing at his wrist-watch, "you are dismissed. I believe you are on duty in the kitchen now."

* * *

As Bruno and Boots slaved over the serving of breakfast, they were too upset to appreciate the humour of the comments from their classmates in the dining room.

"Hey, Walton, there's a fly in my porridge!"

"Boots, this orange juice tastes like dishwater!"

"Hurry up with those pancakes, Walton!"

"Oh, bus-boy . . ."

"Wash your hands, Bruno. There's going to be an

inspection by the Board of Health."

"What did you guys do to deserve this?"

Bruno and Boots did not have time to talk to each other until they were finally allowed to sit down to breakfast in the kitchen.

"I wish," said Bruno savagely, "that he had just expelled us. That would have been kinder."

"He was right, though," reflected Boots.

"I never said he wasn't right," snapped Bruno. "The Fish is always right around here, even when he's wrong. I just don't like being punished."

"I hope he's not too hard on Chris and Wilbur," said Boots.

"Ha! I'll bet he's warming up the rack right now!"

Boots shook his head. "Why is it that you never learn from punishment, Bruno?"

Bruno laughed. "Maybe it's because I'm completely incorrigible."

* * *

When Mrs. Sturgeon drove home from town through a gloomy, cold rain that afternoon, she was appalled to see Bruno and Boots, equipped with pointed sticks and garbage bags, cleaning litter off the front lawn of the campus. She stopped the car and rolled down the window.

"Bruno, Melvin, what are you doing out in such weather?"

"Mr. Sturgeon's orders, Ma'am," said Bruno. "We're being punished."

"But surely he didn't mean on a day like today!" she protested.

"He said every day," said Bruno. "Probably for the rest of the year."

Boots sneezed violently.

"My goodness, you're getting sick! Go to your room at once and each of you take a hot bath."

"Oh, we haven't got time," explained Bruno. "In a little while we have to report for kitchen duty. But don't worry. After dinner the hot steam from the dishes we have to wash will warm us up."

"Well, you go and change into dry clothing first," she ordered. "I'll explain it to Mr. Sturgeon." She drove off, reflecting that she had a great deal to say to her husband.

She entered the house, wiped her wet feet and removed her raincoat. "William, in all the years I've known you, you have never been so cruel!"

Mr. Sturgeon looked up from his newspaper in surprise. "What have I done?"

"As if you don't know!" she exclaimed angrily. "Bruno Walton and Melvin O'Neal are out on that campus in the pouring rain picking up garbage!"

"They are being punished, Mildred," the Headmaster

told her. "It is an administrative matter and no concern of yours."

"I'll bet it would be a concern to those boys' parents if they could see them now," she snapped. "You ought to be ashamed of yourself!"

"What would you have me do about that tollbooth?" he asked in irritation. "Reward them for their ingenuity? They have to be punished for their own good."

"You're not interested in 'their own good,'" she accused him. "You're just mad because you had such a bad experience last night. Bruno and Melvin didn't hit you over the head. That awful girl did. They didn't ask Miss Scrimmage to shoot at you. And they didn't create the traffic jam. *You* did. Why didn't you remove the tollbooth when you found it? And they certainly didn't make the jack-in-the-box fall on your head. If you had any sense, you'd realize that those boys have been raising all that money for you. They adore you. At least, they used to."

"An administrative matter," repeated Mr. Sturgeon firmly. He had never seen his wife so angry. "When is dinner?"

"I'm not finished yet, William. I have something else to say to you. You're angry with those poor boys for being jealous of York Academy when you yourself are green with envy over Tom Hartley's pool. As for dinner, I haven't yet decided if you're getting any!"

* * *

" 'Fraud is a very bad thing,' " read Bruno aloud. "One, two, three, four, five, six. Six words. Only four thousand nine hundred and ninety-four to go."

"Maybe you could add a few extra 'verys,' " suggested Boots. "Only do it quietly, please. I have my own essay to write."

Bruno sighed. "This is impossible. I can't write with dishpan hands."

Boots yawned in agreement. "What a day! Especially when you dropped all those dishes."

"At least we didn't have to wash those," said Bruno. "Of course, we did have to pick up the pieces." He grinned. "I wonder if we looked pathetic enough for Mrs. Sturgeon this afternoon. I'd be able to take this punishment if I thought The Fish was suffering too."

"Oh, she'll go to bat for us," Boots said, "but he'll give her the old fish-eye. This time even dynamite won't move him. He's really mad."

"Hey," said Bruno, "what do you call a guy who does fraud? A fraudist?"

"An idiot," Boots replied.

Smash!

A large rock came crashing through the window and landed on the floor midway between the two boys.

Before they could react, Cathy Burton burst in

through the window, shrieking unintelligibly. Oblivious to the shattered glass, Diane followed. Other screaming girls poured in. Through what was left of the window, a bewildered Bruno and Boots could see the entire population of Miss Scrimmage's Finishing School for Young Ladies swarming in the direction of Dormitory 3.

"What's going on?" cried Bruno across the room to Boots. The boys were squashed up against opposite walls as their room continued to fill up. Boots's reply was a helpless shrug. Cathy went on gesturing and screaming, but Bruno could not make out what she was trying to tell him.

The door was thrown open and there stood the House Master, staring in horror. "What the . . . ?" He was knocked down and trampled as the howling overflow from 306 surged on into the hall. Still they came through the window.

Boots heard someone yelling "Help!" and realized with some chagrin that it was himself.

Pete Anderson threw his door open.

"Hey!"

He was hurled back onto his bed as some of the girls poured into his room and began milling around, knocking things over.

Other doors began to open and boys ran into the corridor to join the hubbub.

"What in the world . . . ?"

"It's an invasion!"

"Girls?"

"Girls!"

"They've killed Mr. Fudge!"

"It's Walton's fault! He let them in!"

"I've got my hand caught in the door!"

"Then take it out!"

"Ouch!"

"Something must have happened!"

Something had indeed happened. Cathy Burton, her voice almost gone, collapsed into a chair and thrust a piece of paper at Bruno.

Bruno stared at it. It was a letter.

Dear Miss Burton

The D-Lishus Baking Powder Company takes great pleasure in informing you that your recipe for 'The Original Triple-Decker Scrim-Apple Upside-Down Cake' has won first prize in the D-Lishus Bake-Off. I must admit that I was dubious about certain ingredients, notably the horseradish, but the result was a most unusual and delicious cake. Enclosed is a cheque for $3,000. Congratulations.

Mavis Cook

General Supervisor, Bake-Off

"I don't believe it!" Bruno roared delightedly over the din. "Boots! *Boots!*"

"Here I am," came a muffled voice.

"Where?"

"Under the bed," replied Boots. "And I'm not coming out!"

142

"Cathy's won some money!" Bruno exclaimed. "Three thousand dollars!"

Boots scooted out from under his bed. "How? For what?"

"We were baking a cake," Cathy croaked. "Miss Scrimmage was entertaining her sister and we had to bake, so we dumped in the horseradish just to liven up the dessert. Then Diane dropped it on the floor and it became upside-down." She laughed, still hysterical. "They loved it! It was great! So we entered it in the contest. And we won! I've endorsed the cheque over to you! Now Boots doesn't have to go to York Academy!"

"Well . . ." began Boots dubiously.

"Oh no!" said Bruno suddenly. "Boots, if The Fish sees this cheque, we're on our way home! We're not allowed to raise any more money!"

"We don't want it!" cried Boots suddenly. "Go buy yourself a helicopter or something!"

"Shhh! Pipe down!" ordered Bruno. "Of course we want it. We'll just have to get it to the bank without telling The Fish."

"Speak of the devil," whispered Cathy, pointing to the door.

In the doorway, Mr. Sturgeon was kneeling over the prostrate body of Mr. Fudge, the House Master.

"See you," said Cathy. She grabbed Diane by the arm and they made an ungraceful exit through the broken window. By this time all the girls had fled the building and were stampeding across the lawn towards their own school.

* * *

"What do you *mean* your girls never left their beds?" demanded Mr. Sturgeon. "Miss Scrimmage, I saw them with my own eyes! . . . Yes, I *was* wearing my glasses at the time! They wrecked one of my dormitories! I have a House Master with a broken nose and so many bruises that he had to be taken to the hospital! And a student with three broken fingers! . . . They are *not* delicate young ladies! They are vandals! . . . Yes, vandals! They threw a boulder through a window! . . . No, I don't know why! They're like the plague! There's no reason for it! . . . Yes, of course I have proof! The damage! What they did to . . . ."

He stared at the receiver. "Mildred, the barracuda hung up on me!"

"Now, dear," soothed his wife. "I suspect you've hung up on her often enough."

The Headmaster crashed his fist into his palm. "Walton and O'Neal are at the bottom of this!" he said firmly.

"How could they be? You said the rock and the broken glass were on the inside of the room. That means the window was broken from the outside. Those poor boys aren't always to blame, you know."

Mr. Sturgeon nodded wearily. "I suppose you're right."

* * *

"The Original Triple-Decker Scrim-Apple Upside-Down Cake!" exclaimed Bruno gleefully.

"With horseradish," added Boots. "We should have known they'd come up with something like that. Three thousand dollars! How are we going to get it to the bank without The Fish finding out about it?"

"Same way we do everything we're not supposed to," said Bruno. "We sneak out under cover of darkness."

"Bruno, people who visit banks at two o'clock in the morning are usually burglars," Boots reminded him.

"Oh," said Bruno. "That does raise a little problem, doesn't it? Well, we'll sit on the cheque for a while until I figure out a way. We sure can't go until we ditch this punishment. No time." He leaned back with a great sigh of contentment. "We have over seventy-five hundred dollars."

"It's a long way from twenty-five thousand," said Boots mournfully.

* * *

Three days after the riot, Mr. Sturgeon was in his office

when he received a telephone call from Mr. Hartley of York Academy.

"Hello there, Hartley. To what do I owe the honour of this call? . . . I beg your pardon? . . . Well, I'm sorry if we happen to be poor competition for your swim team, but my boys cannot accept your kind offer to use your pool. They are asleep at that hour . . ."

A pencil in Mr. Sturgeon's hand suddenly snapped in two.

"The parents of some of *our* boys, you say? Visiting you? Anderson? Jones? *O'Neal?* Well, I'm sure the parents will do what is best for their sons. Parents have every right to choose the school that their children will attend . . . Yes, thank you for calling, Hartley, but we at Macdonald Hall have much more important things to do — like maintaining our high academic standing. We don't want to slip to second place just for the sake of a little splashing around. Goodbye, Hartley."

He slammed the receiver down hard and clicked on his intercom. "Mrs. Davis, send the messenger for Bruno Walton and Melvin O'Neal."

The truth of what had been going on was suddenly crystal clear to him. Here were these boys trying to save Macdonald Hall, trying to keep from losing their friends to York Academy, trying the only way they knew how to stay together, and he, their Headmaster, had accused them of the low motive of jealousy. Certainly there was jealousy present, but there was also something much,

much more. He felt a twinge of shame.

It took more than half an hour for the office messenger to locate Bruno and Boots, as they were off picking up litter in a remote corner of the campus.

"You sent for us, sir?" said Bruno as they entered the office.

"Yes. You have taken your punishment well and have performed your duties satisfactorily. I have decided to lift your punishment as of now."

"The essay too?" Bruno asked hopefully.

"I still want the essay," said Mr. Sturgeon. "I want it to be clear to you that what you almost did might have adversely affected your whole lives."

"Yes, sir. Thank you, sir," chorused Bruno and Boots gratefully.

Did someone mention money?

"Is it ever good to be on this side of the counter!" exclaimed Bruno, enjoying his dinner.

Boots nodded. "The last three days were pure torture. All we have to do now is get the fraud essays finished."

"Yes," Bruno agreed. "And we'd better hurry because we've got to figure out a way to raise the rest of the money."

Boots pounded a fist on the table. "Has your mind finally jumped its one track?" he shouted. "We are *never* going to raise all that money!"

"Money?" said a voice at the next table. "Did someone mention money?"

Bruno and Boots turned to see George Wexford-Smyth III regarding them with great interest.

"We've been trying to raise money for a pool," Bruno told him. "I wouldn't expect you to understand that. It's vulgar."

George picked up his yogurt and came over to join

them. "Money, especially in vast quantities, is never vulgar," he said. "Why don't you tell me all about it?"

"Where have *you* been?" asked Boots. "Don't you know about the swimming pool?" George looked mystified. "The budget won't allow us to build a pool, and we're in danger of losing students to York Academy because of it. That's why we've been trying to raise twenty-five thousand dollars — so we can beat those turkeys in the next swim meet and keep our fathers happy."

"You mean," said George, "all the horrid things that have been going on around the campus were for money?"

Bruno and Boots nodded.

"Well, that makes it different," declared George. "How much did you raise?"

"About seventy-five hundred," said Bruno.

"Hmmm. And you need twenty-five thousand. That shouldn't be difficult."

"What?"

"My dear Bruno," said George. "Didn't Melvin tell you that I am a financial giant?"

"It's true!" exclaimed Boots breathlessly.

"Okay," said Bruno. "But how are you going to take seventy-five hundred dollars and turn it into twenty-five thousand?"

"With considerable ease," said George smugly. "The stock market, of course. I happen to have an inside tip on a mining stock. If you will give me your money, I will invest it for you."

"Hold on just a minute," said Bruno. "I don't know much about the stock market, but if you can make money, you can also lose money. What if we buy and the stock goes down?"

George stiffened. "My stocks never go down."

Boots nodded. "That's true too."

"Okay," said Bruno, "even if we trusted you, there's still a problem. The money is in a special bank account."

"In whose name is this account?" asked George.

"Ours," replied Bruno.

George shrugged expressively. "Then I fail to see your problem. Go and withdraw the money at once. The stock market will not wait, you know."

"We can't touch that money!" exclaimed Boots. "The Fish would slaughter us!"

George smiled. "Mr. Sturgeon would have to find out about it before he could become angry. And when he does find out, it will be because you have all that money to give him."

"My view exactly," said Bruno enthusiastically. "Boots, this is a really cool guy! Why wasn't I told about him?"

"You *were* told," said Boots, "and you *know* what I told you. Bruno if we lose that money, The Fish will kill us for sure!"

Bruno ignored him. "George, how much time do we have to get to the bank?"

"There should be a week or two," George calculated, "but it is usually good to buy earlier. Don't delay too long. Contact me when you have the money." He left them.

"Bruno, are you crazy?" Boots cried. "How can you even consider putting money that doesn't belong to us into the hands of that crackpot?"

"You're the one who told me that that crackpot never loses," said Bruno. "So what's the problem?"

"If you can't see the problem, you're as crazy as he is!" Boots shouted. "You also need *my* signature at the bank, and I'm not signing!"

"Then you're going to be a turkey," said Bruno. "As a matter of fact, you're going to be worse than a turkey because you could have saved yourself and you didn't!"

"Better a turkey than a dead duck!" Boots insisted. "There's no way I'm signing over seventy-five hundred dollars for George to play with."

"How about five thousand?" said Bruno hopefully.

"No," said Boots firmly.

"Well, what about Cathy's three thousand?" suggested Bruno. "The Fish doesn't even know about that, so he can't possibly find out it's missing."

"No!" said Boots.

"You know," said Bruno, "you don't have the right to decide this thing for guys like Pete Anderson who really want to stay here at the Hall. Just because you don't have the belly for it doesn't mean the other guys don't. The Fish said this bank account was a great responsibility. Well, it is. It's our responsibility to poll all the guys — and all the girls too — to find out what they want us to do with their money."

"You know darn well they'd want us to invest it," said Boots angrily.

"Well, then, that's what we have to do — morally," said Bruno. "The question is how much."

"No more than fifty dollars," said Boots.

"That would be a waste of time," said Bruno. "I tend to lean towards a thousand."

"All right," sighed Boots, "a hundred."

"Seven hundred and not a penny less," argued Bruno.

"Two, then," said Boots.

"Ridiculous."

"Two fifty?"

"It's a deal!" said Bruno, much too quickly.

Boots grinned despite his fears. They were friends again.

* * *

The following morning, the Ralph's Laundry truck that picked up and delivered at Macdonald Hall twice a week went slowly down the driveway with its load of dirty laundry. As it was about to turn out onto the highway, the engine coughed once, sputtered and ground to a halt. The driver checked the gas guage. Empty. He left his truck and began walking back to the Faculty Building.

Inside the truck, under a mound of rumpled sheets, Bruno nudged Boots.

"Why are we stopping? We can't be there yet."

"I don't know," said Boots. "This was a terrible idea in the first place."

"Well, how else are we going to get to the bank?" asked Bruno. "We can't very well ask The Fish to give us a lift. He revoked our punishment, but he sure didn't say anything about fund-raising. Why don't you look out the window and see where we are?"

"Not me," said Boots fervently. "If I look out that window, I'll see The Fish looking back in at me."

"All right, I'll look." Bruno scrambled out from under the sheets and crept on all fours to the window in the back door of the panel truck. "Oh no!" he groaned. "We never left the Hall. The truck must have broken down or something. We're sitting at the end of the driveway."

"That means we're in full view of the whole campus!" Boots wailed. "We can't get out! Someone's bound to see us!"

"Shhh! They don't know we're in here yet," warned Bruno. "Stop yelling."

"What are we going to do?" Boots insisted.

"We'll have to wait it out," decided Bruno. "Maybe they'll fix the truck and we can still get to the bank."

Forty-five long minutes passed. The two boys sat in miserable silence, listening to shouts from the nearby soccer field and far-off screams from the girls' field-hockey team at Miss Scrimmage's.

" 'Maybe they'll fix the truck,' " Boots mimicked finally. "And maybe they won't! How are we going to get out of here?"

"Shhh! Someone's coming!" whispered Bruno sharply. "Get down!"

The back door opened and a huge laundry bag was tossed inside. It landed on top of Boots.

"Oof!"

"Ralph?" queried the voice of Wilbur Hackenschleimer. "Is that you, Ralph?"

"No," said Boots. "There's nobody here but us laundry."

"Wilbur!" exclaimed Bruno, poking his head out from under the pile. "We're saved!"

A few minutes later, carrying two large laundry bags, one under each arm, Wilbur Hackenschleimer walked away from the laundry truck in the direction of Dormitory 3.

* * *

"This sure was a great idea of Cathy's," said Bruno

with enthusiasm. He and Boots were lying flat on the floor in the back of Miss Scrimmage's black pick-up truck.

"I thought we'd had enough excitement for one day," said Boots nervously. "I hope no one saw us sneak over here."

"They were all at lunch," said Bruno. "No one was around to see us."

"I wish I was at lunch right now," said Boots. "I'm starving. We spent breakfast in a laundry truck and now lunch in a pick-up. We'll probably spend dinner in jail."

"Why do you have to be such a pessimist?" asked Bruno. "What can go wrong? Cathy said Miss Scrimmage has to go to the drugstore. The drugstore is right next door to the bank. It's all very simple."

Boots just shook his head.

Cathy and Diane stoood on the front steps of the residence and watched Miss Scrimmage's truck pull out onto the highway.

"Hey!" said Diane. "She's going the wrong way!"

Cathy looked surprised. "Maybe she isn't going to the drugstore."

"But you told Bruno . . ."

"Oh well," Cathy laughed, "so they'll have a nice ride." In the distance, thunder rumbled. "Then again, maybe not."

* * *

At six o'clock the rain was still pouring down. Bruno

and Boots, soaked to the skin and weak with hunger, dragged themselves into the dining hall.

Bruno was livid. "I'll get Cathy Burton for this," he said under his breath, "if it takes me two hundred years!"

" 'What can go wrong?' " Boots mimicked savagely. "Nothing much! Miss Scrimmage can go to the hairdresser, buy a darling new dress, stock up on shotgun shells, lose her purse and spend two hours looking for it — everything *except* go to the drugstore."

Both boys picked up trays and got into the cafeteria line, eyeing the food ravenously. Boots sneezed. Bruno coughed and wheezed.

"My goodness, how did you get so wet?" said the elderly lady who was serving dinner.

"It's a long story, Ma'am," said Bruno. "May I please have lots of everything?"

Boots sneezed again. Both boys were shaking with chills.

"You're both sick! Go to the infirmary at once!"

"The infirmary?" asked Boots meekly. "No food?"

"You'll have something there," insisted the lady. "Straight to the infirmary, now. Hurry, before you get worse!"

Bruno and Boots moaned in harmony and obeyed. It was not long before they were propped up in adjacent beds in the infirmary, downing steaming bowls of cream of wheat with great relish.

"You know," said Bruno between enthusiastic slurps, "this may have been a blessing in disguise."

Boots gagged. "Double pneumonia and a bowl of mush! Some blessing! What are you talking about?"

"Well, look at it this way," explained Bruno. "We're not really sick, and tomorrow morning they'll release us. They'll think we're in class, and our teachers will think we're in the infirmary. That'll leave us free to — "

"Go to the bank," finished Boots without much spirit.

* * *

Early the next morning Bruno and Boots stepped outside the infirmary building, took a quick look around and sprinted for the wooded area that lined the eastern perimeter of the campus. When they reached the cover of the trees, they slowed to a walk.

"What time is it?" asked Bruno.

Boots consulted his watch. "Quarter after seven," he replied. "When does that school bus come by?"

"In about twenty minutes," said Bruno. "We'd better hurry."

"Bruno, it's a little kids' school bus. How are we going to pass for little kids? The driver will kick us off."

"No, he won't," said Bruno. "Just leave everything to me."

"I left everything to you yesterday," moaned Boots, "and I had a wonderful day!"

In ten minutes they arrived at the bus stop and

slipped into line with a crowd of young children. As they filed onto the bus, the driver stared and then burst out laughing.

"Big for your age, aren't you?" he asked.

"I failed grade three six times," Bruno grinned back hopefully.

"You guys from Macdonald Hall use this like your own private bus," said the driver. "All right. Take a seat."

Bruno glanced triumphantly at Boots. They were on their way.

When the bank manager arrived to open his bank on the stroke of ten that morning, he found Bruno and Boots asleep on the front step. They had been there since eight o'clock.

Bruno deposited Cathy's cheque to the Macdonald Hall account, then began to fill out a withdrawal slip.

"You know," he said, "Two-fifty isn't very much. Why don't we make it five hundred?"

"No chance!" said Boots firmly.

"Four-fifty then?"

"Bruno, we've been through this before! Two-fifty or nothing!"

"Four hundred? That's a nice round figure."

"All right!" cried Boots in despair. "Three hundred! It's a round figure too, and there's a hundred dollars less of our necks on the line!"

Both signed the withdrawal slip. Boots' hand was

shaking. Bruno pocketed three crisp hundred dollar bills and turned to Boots.

"Now we go home."

"How do we get there?" asked Boots.

Bruno's jaw dropped. "Hmmm. Good question. I guess we walk."

"Walk!" exclaimed Boots. "It's seven miles back to the Hall!"

"Then we'd better get started," said Bruno. "I want to get this money to George."

* * *

"Three hundred dollars?" exclaimed George Wexford-Smyth III in disbelief. "Surely you jest! You told me you had seventy-five."

"My business partner is very cautious," said Bruno. "This will have to do for a start."

"My dear Bruno," said George patiently. "The first rule of high finance is that it takes money to make money."

"First let's see how the investment goes," said Bruno. "There's plenty more where this came from."

Boots looked sick. "You take care of that, George! Don't lose it!"

"I have no intention of losing it," George smiled. "I shall invest it wisely." He turned to walk away.

"Hey, wait a minute," said Bruno. "What's the name of our stock?"

"Lorelei Mining," replied George.

* * *

Three days after the investment had been made, Bruno Walton's head was buried deep in the financial section of the morning paper. Elmer Drimsdale and Boots O'Neal hung over his shoulder, anxious for news.

"Here it is," said Bruno. "And look! It's gone up two cents!"

"We are ten dollars richer," said Elmer.

"But we could have made a fortune if we'd invested the whole thing!" Bruno exclaimed.

"$251.68 precisely," said Elmer.

"See?" said Bruno to Boots. "You're holding us back!"

"I'm not holding you back," replied Boots. "I'm keeping you sane. It could just as easily have gone down two cents. Or more."

"But it didn't," said Bruno. "And it won't. George knows what he's doing. His father made millions this way. That's why we're going to the bank to get the rest of the money."

"No way!" exclaimed Boots. "It's too big a risk!"

"If the rest of the guys knew _you_ cost them $240, they'd wring your neck," insisted Bruno. "We can't afford _not_ to invest _now_. Isn't that right, Elmer?"

"From a purely mathematical viewpoint," said Elmer, "it would appear that you should invest further.

However, I have not gone into the probabilities of the situation — "

"You see?" interrupted Bruno triumphantly. "We've got to invest the rest of that money!"

"Not all of it," said Boots anxiously. "Maybe another three hundred."

"Twice small potatoes is still small potatoes," said Bruno. "And the shares are going to cost us two cents more now."

"Well, maybe four hundred then," agreed Boots.

"Five thousand," said Bruno evenly.

"Come on, Bruno, be reasonable!" Boots wailed. "Don't you understand what's at stake here?"

"I sure do," said Bruno. "You're at stake here — and Pete Anderson — and the honour of Macdonald Hall. There's to be no more fooling around with pennies. You of all people should be willing to take a chance, since one is all you have."

Boots swallowed hard. "A thousand dollars," he gasped.

"Done," said Bruno, rather pleased with himself. "If we hurry, we can go out with Ralph."

"Ralph? But Bruno — "

"Don't worry," said Bruno, "lightning seldom strikes twice in the same laundry truck."

"Actually," said Elmer, "the odds are — "

"Some other time," said Bruno. "We're in a hurry."

* * *

"Your decision to invest further was a wise one," said George over dinner that day. "Naturally, it would have been better to have invested the whole amount at sixty cents as I did with the first three hundred. You now own 2,112 shares of Lorelei Mining, presently worth roughly $1,300. Please invest the rest shortly. The secret of making money in the stock market is to buy low and sell high."

"Yeah, well let's see how this does before we put in any more," said Bruno. "Besides, I have to fight with my partner here over every cent of it."

George nodded sympathetically. "Haggling is so vulgar," he agreed.

* * *

As word of the investment got around among the students, a new kind of insanity broke out at Macdonald Hall — love of learning. Specifically, of mathematics. Mr. Stratton, head of the math department, could scarcely believe his good fortune when a delegation of boys, headed by Bruno and Boots, appeared in his office to request that all math courses include an immediate in-depth study of the stock exchange.

Comic magazines disappeared and were replaced by copies of *The Financial Post*. The few boys who subscribed to Toronto newspapers were literally mobbed each day when the papers arrived, by boys anxious for a glance at the financial pages. Boys who had trouble with their times tables now spoke with ease of "blue chips," "mergers," "speculation" and "marginal buying." The name Lorelei Mining was on everybody's lips.

Strangest of all, George Wexford-Smyth III, ignored, ridiculed and friendless, had become the most popular boy on campus. He was never seen without an admiring crowd, and there was a waiting list of boys who wanted to see him and his teletype machine for financial consultation.

Five days after the second investment had been made, Bruno and Boots arrived at George's room in a high state of excitement. George let them in.

"How's it going?" asked Boots anxiously.

"Quite an impressive gain," said George. "Last night Lorelei closed at sixty-nine cents. You've made about a hundred and fifty dollars."

"Is that all?" said Boots. It seemed to him that they were taking a very big risk for a very small return.

"Had you invested the whole amount," replied George reproachfully, "you would have made over a thousand."

Bruno grabbed Boots by the arm. "Come on! We've got to go to the bank and get the rest of the money!"

"Only another thousand!" begged Boots pathetically.

"Whatever," said Bruno.

* * *

With yet another thousand dollars invested, the stock market fever at Macdonald Hall was becoming even more intense. Lorelei Mining became the only topic of conversation.

It had become George's custom over the days to consult his teletype machine before coming to the dining room for lunch. On this particular day, some ten days after the third investment, he entered the room, stood in the doorway and cleared his throat softly. All eyes turned to him and silence fell. Mr. Sturgeon himself could not have commanded order so quickly.

"Lorelei presently stands at eighty-one cents a share," he announced briskly. "Macdonald Hall holdings now total $2,884.41."

There was applause from everyone except Boots. His eyes were strangely haunted.

It was two o'clock in the morning when Bruno was suddenly hauled out of bed by his frantic roommate.

"Bruno, wake up! Wake up!"

Bruno was in a daze. "What? What? What?"

Boots's anxious white face hovered over him. "We have to buy that stock, Bruno! Today!"

"Today hasn't started yet," mumbled Bruno. "Wake me up when it does."

"Bruno, the *stock!*" Boots repeated. *"We've got to get the rest of the money and invest it right away!"*

Bruno woke up instantly. "Now you're talking!" he said with a grin.

* * *

Ralph Colacci pulled his laundry truck into the small shopping centre parking lot, got out and headed for the diner for a cup of coffee. In the back of his truck, a sheet moved.

"We're here," it said.

Boots O'Neal appeared from under a mountain of towels. "Let's go," he said.

Bruno and Boots scrambled stealthily out of the truck, whipped past the diner, past the drugstore and into the bank.

"This time all of it," said Bruno as he began filling out a withdrawal slip. "$5,250.29."

"Let's leave the twenty-nine cents," suggested Boots nervously.

"Good idea," said Bruno. "Then we'll still have the account here, all ready for when we bring in the big boodle."

They presented the slip to the teller who prepared a bank draft for the money. Bruno pocketed the precious piece of paper and they began the long walk back to Macdonald Hall. Both boys were very quiet as they trudged along the soft shoulder of the highway.

To sell or not to sell

Bruno kicked the door of room 109 with great determination.

"George!" he shouted. "George, open up and let me in so I can kill you!"

It was a week after the entire Macdonald Hall pool fund had been invested, and Lorelei Mining had taken a sudden alarming dip.

George, impeccably dressed in suede and cashmere, opened the door. "Yes? Bruno — Melvin — you require something of me?"

"The whole campus requires something of you!" exclaimed Bruno. "Your head! Lorelei's dropped down to sixty-five cents! *We're losing money!*"

"Simply a minor setback," said George calmly.

"Your minor setback has cost us fifteen hundred dollars!" cried Boots in agony. "We're going to lose! We're going to lose it all! And then what will we tell The Fish?"

"There is silver in that mine," George assured them. "I have it from the most reputable firm of geologists in Canada. It is simply a matter of time."

"You mean it's going to start going up soon?" demanded Bruno hopefully.

George smiled confidently. "Trust me," he said.

* * *

Three days later, Bruno and Boots were wishing with all their hearts that they had not put their trust in George. Lorelei now stood at fifty-eight cents per share.

"We're doomed," moaned Boots dismally, unable to concentrate on his homework. "The guys'll kill us. The girls'll kill us. The Fish'll kill us. In fact, I think I'll kill myself and save them the trouble."

"Twenty-two hundred down the drain," mourned Bruno. "That George! Why didn't you warn me about him?"

"I *did* warn you! You wouldn't listen! You *never* listen! He's a lunatic!"

"George still says we should hold on and we'll make our money," said Bruno. "But it sure doesn't look as if our stock is going to go up."

"I say we sell," said Boots, "while we still have some money. It makes sense to try and salvage something out of this mess."

"Well, I don't know . . ." Bruno began. He glanced

out the window. "Hey, what's going on outside? All the guys are out there."

"They're probably gathering a mob to run us out of town," Boots predicted miserably.

"Look!" exclaimed Bruno. "They've got George! We'd better get out there and protect him! Everybody's mad enough to kill him!"

"Just remember that we're culprits number two and three," said Boots. "I don't want to go out there. Let George protect himself!"

Bruno opened the window. "Listen to that!"

From across the road came the rhythmic chanting of female voices: "We love George! We love George!"

Bruno and Boots exchanged a quick, confused glance before leaping out of their open window to join the crowd. They were met by a jubilant Pete Anderson. With him was Elmer Drimsdale, his neat black tie flapping in the breeze, his glasses awry.

"Don't be too hard on George!" shouted Bruno over the general din.

"Hard on him?" laughed Pete. "We're going to make him king!" And he ran back into the crowd which was, by this time, carrying George high in the air.

Bruno grabbed Elmer by his thin shoulders. "Elmer, what's going on here?"

"Well, I'm not certain exactly," said Elmer, "but I believe it has something to do with some men finding a lot of silver in our mine."

At that instant, Wilbur Hackenschleimer thundered up and thrust a copy of the financial page of the evening paper into Bruno's astonished face. The headline read: *Rich Vein Discovered at Lorelei Mine.*

Bruno threw his head back and howled with delight.

Breathlessly, Boots read the article. *"A half hour after the stock market closed today, it was revealed that mining operations at Lorelei Mining Inc. have uncovered one of the richest silver deposits ever found in Canada. A company spokesman . . .* Bruno, we're going to be *rich!"*

Bruno was ecstatic. "I knew George would come through! He's not a crackpot! He's a genius! George! George!" He ran off towards the hero of the day. Boots followed.

The mob carrying George set him down before the president and vice-president of the fund-raising committee.

"Well, George," said Bruno, "what do you think of that?"

George was as composed as ever. "I fail to understand why everyone is so surprised," he said. "I told you about all this some time ago."

"Yes, but we didn't believe you!" blurted Boots.

Bruno clamped a hand over Boots's mouth. "He's excited. He doesn't know what he's saying. We believe! We believe!"

"May I ask what is going on here?" said a quiet voice behind them.

Silence fell. All eyes turned to Mr. Sturgeon who stood a few yards away watching them.

"Lights-out," said the Headmaster, "is exactly three minutes from now. I fail to see why no one appears to respect the rules of this institution." A puzzled frown creased his forehead as the last "We love George" died away from across the road. "You will return to your rooms immediately and go to bed."

As the crowd began to disperse, Bruno grinned at George. "How did it feel to be part of one of our riots?"

George almost grinned back. "Actually," he said, "I found that vulgar display of emotion rather exhilarating. However, I certainly hope I do not become ill from all this night air. Very bad for my sinuses, you understand."

* * *

The next day Lorelei mining made an enormous gain, closing at $1.04 per share. There was much jubilation at Macdonald Hall; their stock had recovered from its slump and shot up so that the school's holdings were now worth more than ten thousand dollars.

All through the week that followed, the students of Macdonald Hall waited and, as George put it, "watched their hard-earned money grow and grow." Glowing reports continued to be published about the quality of the silver strike at Lorelei. The stock continued to rise. When the stock market closed on Friday, the shares were worth $1.73 each.

"$17,372.66," announced Elmer Drimsdale excitedly. "That's a fortune!"

"You know," said Boots, "maybe we should sell out. How high can it go?"

"He may have a point there," said Bruno to George. "We didn't make nearly as much money on Thursday and Friday as we did at the beginning of the week. Maybe it isn't going to go up any more."

"When the time has come to sell," George said calmly, "I shall tell you. Trust me."

The next day the financial papers published further reports on Lorelei Mining. Not only was the silver of high quality, but the find was apparently extensive. Two minor veins had been uncovered. By the time the stock market closed, Lorelei Mining was worth $2.02 per share.

"Sell!" Boots begged. "For pity's sake, let's sell! We have over twenty thousand dollars!"

"But you require twenty-five," said George. "And you will have it. You must be patient. These things don't happen overnight."

At the end of the week the discovery of yet another silver vein nudged Lorelei Mining up to $2.57 per share.

A half-demented Pete Anderson delivered the news at lunch on Friday. "We did it!" he screamed, waving a newspaper in the air. "We broke twenty-five thousand!"

Pandemonium broke loose in the dining hall. Napkins flew through the air and boys began running around congratulating each other wildly. Elmer Drimsdale was so happy he burst into tears. Wilbur Hackenschleimer, for the first time in his life, was too overcome to eat. Chris Talbot ran around the dining hall pounding people on the back and gibbering incoherently. Mark Davies, puffed up with pride, strutted around as though he himself were responsible for the great accomplishment. Sidney Rampulsky overturned his chair and whacked his head on the edge of the table, knocking himself unconscious. Boots just sat and savoured the taste of victory.

Bruno's voice was the loudest. "That's it!" he screamed. "We did it! We've got more than enough! Sell! Sell! Sell!"

"What about an adjoining sauna?" asked George calmly. "And our pool should be bigger and better than York Academy's. They are so vulgar." And he would not sell.

Macdonald Hall held on. All through the next two weeks the financial papers published reports on the phenomenon that was Lorelei Mining. Seldom had a stock gained so much in so short a time. Mining operations were not only fairly inexpensive but extremely profitable as well. And yet another sizable vein of silver had been discovered.

When Lorelei closed at $3.21 per share, Bruno Walton was no longer in a selling mood. "After the pool," he was telling everybody, "we can build a planetarium, renovate the dormitories, set up a broadcasting studio and maybe build a museum. Why, we'll buy York Academy and throw all the turkeys out!"

George Wexford-Smyth III said one word: "Sell."

Bruno was aghast. "What do you mean sell? We've only been in this for a few weeks! Now we can start to make some real money!"

"My inside information says that there is one enormous vein, one rather sizable vein and three smaller ones," said George. "The stock should be peaking just about now. It will level off and then slowly begin to decline until it reaches a normal level for a stock of this nature. Tomorrow I shall call my broker. We sell."

The next morning George telephoned his stock broker who liquidated the Macdonald Hall holdings for a grand total of $32,234.82 and dispatched a courier to deliver the cheque to his young clients.

True to George's prediction, Lorelei's next gain was extremely insignificant. The stock indeed appeared to be levelling off.

"You were right," said Bruno. "We sold out at the right time."

"Naturally," said George, fanning himself with the cheque.

"You know something, George?" remarked Boots. "You're not such a creep after all."

"Indeed," smiled George sincerely, "you two are not quite so disgusting as I had originally thought either. Still a little vulgar, mind you . . ."

* * *

"Dear son," read Boots aloud from the letter he had just received from his mother. *"I have this vague feeling that you are worried about being taken out of Macdonald Hall and sent to a school with a more extensive athletic program. Your father and I have discussed this and have decided that we'd rather have you happy than an Olympic athlete. We are also very pleased that you seem to be getting so much joy out of your classes lately. We love hearing from you twice a day. Keep it up.*

Love, Mom."

"No gobble-gobble?" Bruno questioned.

Boots nodded hysterically. "I can stay! I can stay! I can *stay!*"

"Everyone can stay," said Bruno with great satisfaction.

For he's a jolly good fellow!

"Mildred, I cannot imagine what this is about!" said Mr. Sturgeon, knotting his tie. "I am not accustomed to being called to assembly by my students. If it has anything to do with fund-raising, I promise you I shall wring their necks!"

"I have no idea what it means," his wife said, putting the finishing touches on her hair-do. "Bruno and Melvin showed up at the door at four o'clock and invited us to a special assembly after dinner. I've been phoning around to the faculty and it seems that everyone is invited, but no one knows what it's all about."

"If Walton and O'Neal are behind it," the Headmaster said sourly, "it's probably a new fund-raising scheme. We shall all be held for ransom."

"Hurry now," she said, "or we'll be late. We're to meet Miss Scrimmage outside the auditorium in five minutes."

"Miss Scrimmage? Why is *she* invited?"

"Well, I don't know, dear. Let's go and find out."

* * *

Mr. Sturgeon's fears were confirmed as he, his wife and Miss Scrimmage were seated in the front row of the auditorium. On the platform were Bruno and Boots, Wilbur, Chris, Elmer and Mark — the entire fund-raising committee. To make matters more perplexing, the extra boy on the stage, George Wexford-Smyth III, was known to be generally disliked. Where did he fit in? What was going on here?

Because of the presence of Miss Scrimmage's girls, the auditorium was packed to overflowing. Students were sitting on the floor in the aisles.

Bruno stepped up to the microphone and cleared his throat.

"Honoured guests, fellow students," he began, and it was apparent that he had rehearsed very carefully. "We are gathered here this evening to celebrate a memorable event. I would now like to call Mr. Sturgeon to the platform, as I have a few brief words to address to him."

As Mr. Sturgeon joined him at the microphone, Bruno reached into his pocket and produced enough paper for a two-hour speech. There were loud groans from the audience and several elaborate yawns. Mr. Sturgeon silenced everyone with one cold look. He felt like the leading actor in a farce and was not in a particularly good mood.

"Mr. Sturgeon," Bruno began, "I — we — George — silver — here, sir!" His face flaming red and his speech forgotten, Bruno whipped an envelope out of his pocket and thrust it into the Headmaster's hand.

"Great speech!" Cathy Burton cheered from the back row.

Mystified, Mr. Sturgeon opened the envelope and removed the contents. He found himself holding a cheque in the amount of $32,234.82. There was a long silence. The Headmaster stared from the cheque to Bruno and back to the cheque again.

"It's for a pool, sir," Bruno stammered, "with extra dressing rooms for the girls because they helped. And a sauna. And *please,* sir, could it be bigger than York Academy's pool? Even if it's just a little bigger?"

An unfamiliar expression came over the Headmaster's face. He took out his handkerchief and blew his nose loudly. In the front row Mrs. Sturgeon was dabbing at her eyes with a lace hanky and trying to quiet Miss Scrimmage, who was sobbing uncontrollably. The cheering from the boys was deafening, and the girls were standing up and dancing wherever they could find room to put a foot down. Confetti flew like snow, and several boys waved hand-made victory flags.

"Aren't you happy, sir?" Bruno shouted over the din.

"Very happy indeed," said Mr. Sturgeon. "But where on earth did you get so much money?"

"It's a very long story, sir," said Bruno hesitantly.

"Are you sure you want to hear it?"

"Not at all sure. But perhaps I'd better. After the assembly, I want to see you and O'Neal privately in my office."

"Yes, sir," said Bruno. "And we'd better bring George."

"Wexford-Smyth III?" asked Mr. Sturgeon. "I was under the impression that you did not even associate with him."

"George?" said Bruno in surprise. "Why, he's our best friend. He may look like a creep, but you can't judge a book by its cover."

"Very true," Mr. Sturgeon nodded.

Boots approached them. "Sir," he said, "all the ruckus has died down now. Would you like to say a few words?"

Mr. Sturgeon nodded, blew his nose once again and addressed the assembly.

"When I was called here tonight, I recall thinking that if this assembly had anything to do with fund-raising, heads would roll. Fund-raising has made this an interesting semester, to say the least. And now we are to have a pool." There was much stamping and whistling. "Getting the pool has been the achievement of every boy and girl in this auditorium. For this reason, the name over the door of our pool will read: *Students' pool.*" Again he was interrupted by wild cheering. "I don't know how you did it," he went on. "I am shortly to be filled in on the details. I only want to say thank you and to let you know that I am very proud of every one of you."

To the sound of hundreds of young voices singing "For He's a Jolly Good Fellow," Mr. Sturgeon left the stage and rejoined his wife.

"Well, William," she said happily, "what do you think of that?"

"A telephone," said Mr. Sturgeon abstractedly. "We need a telephone in the sauna." His eyes took on a wicked gleam. "I want to phone Hartley from there. And I must also mention to him how lucky he is that his water bill will be so much smaller than ours."

"Oh, William!" she laughed. "You *are* pleased!"

He nodded. "And I can also invite Hartley's students to use our sauna — between the hours of two and three in the morning on nights when there is a full moon!" His face grew grave. "Of course, first I have to find out where they got that money and whether or not we have to give it back."

*　*　*

Bruno, Boots and George sat in three comfortable swivel chairs facing their Headmaster across his desk.

"It's all very simple, sir," said Bruno. "George took our seventy-five hundred dollars and invested it in the stock market for us."

"But you didn't have seventy-five hundred," protested Mr. Sturgeon, mystified.

"Yes, sir," said Bruno. "But Cathy made horseradish cake and won three thousand dollars for us."

"Oh," said Mr. Sturgeon oddly, "I see."

"So," Bruno went on, "George invested our money."

The Headmaster stared at him. "I received reports that you and O'Neal had missed a few classes. I assume that would be trips to the bank and other financial transactions?"

"Yes, sir," Bruno admitted.

Mr. Sturgeon held his head. "Don't you two realize — and you too, Wexford-Smyth — that you had no moral right to touch that money? I entrusted you with the responsibility of that bank account."

"Yes, sir," said Bruno, "and we more than tripled it."

"Yes," said Mr. Sturgeon, "but you might just as easily have lost it."

George sat bolt upright in his chair. "Impossible, sir!" he exclaimed. "There is a science to the stock market. I had inside information on Lorelei Mining from a reputable firm of geologists."

"Lorelei Mining?" repeated the Headmaster. *"That* was your investment? You knew about Lorelei Mining before it happened? Why, that was the biggest — " He caught himself and fell silent.

"Are you very angry, sir?" asked Boots in a small voice.

"Yes — and no," said Mr. Sturgeon. "You see, I am afraid that this experience may have taught you boys that you can do absolutely anything to achieve what you are after. Life is not like that. There are rules. At some time in your lives you will have to give up something you want very badly because the means to get it will hurt someone else. Do you understand?"

"Yes, sir," chorused the three boys.

"As for the money itself," said Mr. Sturgeon with a smile, "I could not be more pleased. I think, under the circumstances, that Wexford-Smyth should be the first person to swim in our pool."

"Oh, no, sir!" said George quickly. "From a hygienic point of view, I feel pools are unsafe. And of course there is the ever-present danger of catching a chill."

"Well, then," said the Headmaster with a trace of amusement in his voice, "the honour should fall to the chairman of the fund-raising committee. Bruno, you should be first in our pool."

Bruno turned deathly white. "Me, sir? Pool, sir? But I don't know how to swim!"

About the Author

Gordon Korman wrote his first book, *This Can't Be Happening at Macdonald Hall*, as a seventh grade English project. By the time Korman had graduated from high school he had written and published five other books including *Go Jump in the Pool!*, *Beware the Fish!*, and *The War with Mr. Wizzle* all available in Apple Paperback editions from Scholastic Inc. Korman in now studying film and screenwriting at New York University. Between semesters he finds time to answer piles of fan mail and make personal appearances across the country.